Mark Foss

Kissing the Damned

The publishers acknowledge the support of the Canada Council for the Arts, the Government of Ontario through the Ontario Media Development Corporation and the Government of Canada through the Book Publishing Industry Development Program for their publishing activities.

This is a work of fiction, and any resemblances to actual people or organizations are coincidental.

I am indebted to Valerie Cousins and Gareth Llewellyn for their editorial support and encouragement in the book's early stages, to Isabel Huggan for helping me find its shape, and, above all, to Richard Taylor for believing in the book enough to push and prod me into discovering new depths, and for cheerleading. I would also like to thank Guy Jobin, who survived the torpedo attack on *HMS Nabob* in 1944, for sharing his experiences. Finally, I am grateful to Wrenna Prest, Mier Prest, Michael Schiesser and Neelama Eyres, who, in their own way, enrich my life beyond words.

Several stories have appeared in sometimes quite different form in *McGill Street Magazine* and *Zygote* and on gritlit.ca.

ISBN 0 7780 1278 6 (hardcover)
ISBN 0 7780 1279 4 (softcover)

Cover art by Henri de Toulouse-Lautrec
Book design by Michael Macklem

Printed in Canada

PUBLISHED IN CANADA BY OBERON PRESS

Contents

For WMG, my parents, and in memory of Robert Miller

The Guest-House

Nicky and I had met in a film studies course in which she was the teacher's assistant. We acknowledged our attraction, but she did not want to jeopardize her position.

"My unavailability attracted you, Murray," she'd said afterwards. "That's why you don't want to move in with me now. It's too easy."

Maybe it was true. For the first two years, during visits to my parents' cottage on the St. Lawrence River near Brockville, I had slipped out of my bedroom window to join Nicky in the guest-house at the back of the garage. For the past two years, since the day Mom had finally made up two beds in the guest-house, our sex life had never recovered. I could only imagine what Nicky's constant availability would do to my libido.

We had just parked the car at the cottage when she'd noticed the missing earring.

"You took it out?"

"He'll think I'm gay. It's not worth the fuss."

"What does it matter what he thinks? You should keep it in."

"What does it matter what you think?"

"Do what you want then. You disappoint me, that's all. For god's sake, you're nearly 30 and you're still afraid of your father."

"I'm not afraid. It's a question of respect for his values."

"Sure, Murray. Whatever."

We scuffled our feet across the dirt road. I turned my head, but she wouldn't look me in the eyes. Her glance went back to my ear.

"It's bleeding. If you put it back in, it might stop the flow."

I touched my ear. A few drops on my finger. I sucked them off.

"It's still bleeding."

I stopped again.

"All right. I'll put the damned thing back in."

"Let me help."

"I can do it myself."

I found the stud in my pocket. After I got it through my ear and secured it, Nicky touched her finger to my lobe. She showed me the tiny speck of blood on her finger, and then sucked it off.

We were halfway across the lawn with our bags.

"Just for fun, why don't I sleep in the cottage and sneak into the guest-house tonight?" I said.

"Because it's juvenile."

"I thought you liked the child-like part of me."

"Child-like, yes. Not childish. There's a difference."

"Says who?"

She let that one go.

"Looks like rain," I said. "You know what that means."

"Murray Lockhart's child comes out to play. Oh boy."

On rainy afternoons at the cottage, just like when I was a kid, Nicky and I played games like Don't Break the Ice and Battleship. She always maintained an ironic detachment, befitting her cultural studies' training. For her, the little man sitting on the block of ice, waiting for the inevitable tap of the hammer that would send him crashing to his doom, signified Existential Man. When I killed the little man, she would spew out the line from the TV commercial—"You broke the ice!"—with postmodern glee. When I said the line, it sounded the same, but I really was eleven years old again, full of childish fervour. She didn't notice the difference, not for years.

While Nicky and I played Battleship, Mom skimmed through old issues of *Women's Day* for new recipes, and Dad sorted through photographs of his war years.

"B15," I said.

"Hit."

"B16."

"Hit and sunk."

She stuck one more plastic torpedo in her aircraft carrier, and then took it off the board.

Dad watched us. He had served on an aircraft carrier with his childhood friend Ted, who had died during a torpedo attack on the *Nabob*.

"It was never like that," he said.

Then he noticed the earring.

"You've got to be kidding," he said. "Virginia, look at this. Our son."

"I think it looks good on him," Nicky said.

Dad shovelled his photos into a box, and left the cottage.

"You've upset your father," Mom said. Then she went back to the kitchen.

"Congratulations," Nicky said. "You just cut loose."

At dinner, Dad picked at his food. He didn't speak. He didn't look at me. After dinner, we turned on the TV, but the remote control for the aerial wasn't working.

Our aerial was atop a twenty-foot metal pole that stood outside the cottage beside the dining-room window. When I was a kid, Dad and I painted numbers on the pole to mark the best reception for the Ottawa and Kingston channels. We were a team. I would stand outside and turn the pole, while Dad would signal from inside when the audio was clear.

"I'll go," I said, looking at Nicky. "Stand here and let me know when you can hear it."

I hadn't touched the pole for years. It felt cold and rust came off in my hands. You had to turn it one way and then back the other so the wires wouldn't get wound too tight. In the dark, I could barely make out the faded numbers, but it didn't matter because we wanted *Saturday Night at the Movies* on TV Ontario, and it wasn't marked on the pole. We never had that channel when I grew up.

Through the window, I saw Nicky on the edge of the sofa. Mom fixed coffee. Dad pouted.

As I turned the pole, the picture started to come in.

Nicky turned to look at the TV, then waved me in.

Then Dad came up from behind Nicky. He shook his head and twirled his finger. Keep tuning, it said.

He stood in front of Nicky, covering up the TV picture as well. Nicky took a few steps back, and then walked out of the room. I heard the front door close on the other side of the cottage. I stood in the dark, hands tight on the pole, following my father's signals.

Nicky fled Ottawa—and me—to pursue graduate studies. A few days after she left, I was at the video store searching for the pilot to the old *Kung Fu* television series. I liked the idea of the soft-spoken priest so perfectly in tune with the universe. I wanted to live vicariously through him for a while. It was a change from writing fundraising letters at Go Postal, Ottawa's all-too-hip direct marketing firm.

I was moving right to left in the K section when I spotted it. My hand reached out, touching a woman's hand, who had been coming down the aisle from the left.

"If you can take the video from my hand," she said, "it will be time for you to leave."

In Nicky's mouth, those words—a twist on a familiar line from the series—would have taken on a wry, knowing tone. But Cassandra said them with true love and affection. I recognized a kindred spirit.

When I grabbed the video, she didn't let go.

We biked back to her apartment, leaving the video encased in plastic while we made love.

For two years we spent four evenings a week together, renting movies and watching reruns. Some nights we made love. Other nights we just stroked each other's bodies, while an old show played in the background. On Saturday mornings, we fought over the TV Guide. While we made dinner, we quizzed each other with lines of dialogue, character impressions or trivia.

But I was getting bored. It was getting more difficult to find a video we hadn't seen. And I missed Nicky's intellectual rigour, her feminist-take on culture, her widespread interests. Cassandra was an administrative assistant in the government with no particular ambition. I also discovered she took mental-health days to watch daytime TV.

At first, she had no interest in spending a weekend at the cottage without cable. That was fine because I wanted to keep her away from my parents. The earring episode had unnerved my father. He had sent an impassioned letter about losing Ted in the war. Seeing me wear an earring, he'd written, brought it all back. It had quashed all of his dreams for me. When I visited, I took the earring out, but the damage had been done. Ted was never far away. Dad reminisced about childhood incidents and their war experiences on the *Nabob*. He was likely to cry, which made me uncomfortable.

Then, perhaps out of boredom with me, Cassandra announced her desire to meet my parents.

"Can you last a whole weekend without cable?" I'd said.

"We can bring videos."

"They're getting ready to close up and drive to Florida. Why don't we wait till the spring?"

"No, let's go now. I want to see this big pole you keep talking about. It will turn me on to see you tune in."

Sometimes she scared me.

It only took fifteen minutes with Cassandra before Dad mentioned Ted.

"We grew up together," Dad said. "He saved my life."

"How?" she said.

"We were walking along the river one winter and the ice gave way. I fell in the hole. If he hadn't been there...."

"Wow."

"Then of course when the torpedo hit, well, I tried to reach him. But there was too much chaos. It was a hell of a mess. Water pouring in, and oil too. It was pitch black."

"So you couldn't reach him. That's so sad."

As tears welled up in Dad's eyes, she put a hand on his shoulder. He squeezed her other hand.

I watched, irritated and jealous. That night, as we got ready for bed, I lashed out.

"Why were you encouraging him? It's fine for you to breeze in for a weekend. I've got to live with this."

"He needs to talk. He needs to get it out."

"You're a clerk, not a therapist."

She grabbed the condom from the night table, still in its wrapper. She shoved it into my palm.

"Time for you to fucking leave."

"I'm sorry."

"Get out."

I sneaked back to my old room in the cottage through the window. A few minutes later, I heard the car. Time for her to leave too.

Paulette and I had been together for six years, living together for four. When we visited the cottage, we always spooned together in one of the twin beds in the guest-house. She liked the privacy: we couldn't hear the floorboards creak when my father visited the bathroom and my parents couldn't hear the bed creak when we made love. It was not private for me. With every shift on the bed, I remembered Nicky's calculated moves and Cassandra's cheerful floppiness. I heard Ted, too. Paulette could escape Ted by retreating to the guest-house, but he followed me out here. He sat on the chair in the darkness, watching, listening, judging.

On Labour Day weekend, I woke first, my face just inches from her hair. My right arm, trapped under her body, tingled. I lay still. I often teased that because she was 38, a year older than I was, she needed her beauty sleep. Our body heat kept us warm, even with the fall chill in the air. Still, my mother had plied us with extra wool blankets. I had taken them, unwilling to let on that Paulette and I crowded into the same bed.

On the other side of the wall, behind the headboard, I heard working sounds: the thud and scrape of tools being used and discarded. Dad's latest project was to place the Sony inside the shell of Grandpa's old RCA. As I listened, I resisted my childhood conditioning to offer help or run away.

Through cracks in the curtains, I sensed a pale sun outside. I had always believed that the stroke of midnight on 31 August turned summer into autumn. Maybe it was because as a child we always packed up on Labour Day weekend, leaving the cottage for the house in Ottawa. I had patches of memories: the Jerry Lewis telethon, cool weather, long pants, the conflicting feelings of loss and anticipation.

Paulette stirred and I removed my lifeless arm from underneath her body. She took my other arm and placed my left hand on her breast.

"I dreamt about having a child again," she said.

"Boy or girl?"

"I'm not sure."

"Who was the father?"

"That's not funny."

"Sorry."

She pushed my hand off her breast.

"I can't wait forever."

Behind the wall, the table-saw warmed up. I tensed, waiting for the blade to bite the wood. I used to hold the weight of large boards while Dad passed them through the saw. Once again, I fought the urge to help. As the wood passed through the blade, the saw screeched, building in intensity until the wood split in two. I fell into silence to avoid another prolonged discussion—Paulette called it the "withdrawal method." Sometimes my silence made her think she'd won, but not this time.

"What do you have against children?"

"We've gone through all this."

"Tell me again."

"They take over your life."

"What life? You've got a new job. You've saving the starving Africans now, but you're not any happier. You just want to fuck and watch TV."

"I don't watch TV as much anymore."

"That's true. You surf the Net instead. But it's the same thing. It's just another screen."

"You want to know the real reason I'm not sure about kids? I don't want to fight over what shows to watch."

She laughed, in spite of herself. As she shifted around to face me, I held her from falling off the narrow bed.

"I suppose we could get another TV," I said.

It was a joke, but when her eyes softened with hope, I regretted the words. I'd kept her dreams alive.

She kissed me, and put her hand between my legs. Nothing. Fear of creating life had sucked the life out of me.

She played with my foreskin.

"Why didn't they get you circumcised?"

"I was born on a Friday night and they wanted to get to the cottage."

She laughed again. "Our child would have a great sense of humour."

"As long as he doesn't try stand-up. It's too risky. Case in point."

"I can fix that."

She slipped off the bed to kneel on the rug, bringing her hands up as if to pray. Her teeth tugged gently on my foreskin just as Dad turned on the table-saw again. I lost all hope, but when the saw shut off, it started to happen. She kept going for a while, then scrambled back into bed on top of me. She tried to kiss me, but I couldn't stand tasting myself in her mouth so I bit into her neck. I was distracted, first by my fear

14

that she didn't really take her pill last night and then by the sound of Dad moving the TVs around in the garage. I was fading so I put on a good show. When I slipped out, she thought I was spent. She kissed my forehead and folded into me. She didn't care about her own orgasms any more, just mine.

We lay on our sides in silence, listening to the grunts as my father fit the Sony inside the RCA. I heard loud static. He'd turned the TV on, probably to see how the picture looked in its new home. The static disappeared, replaced by a chorus of gospel singers. I could hear Dad's voice join them in "Amazing Grace." Without the picture of the TV evangelist to distract me, I was swept away by the singing. We all were, each praying for something else.

Escort

I stood at International Arrivals with a bag of borrowed clothes, waiting for a man I didn't know who was expecting someone else. Frank Chande, the Tanzania field officer for Friends of Africa, was coming for a week of training in project management and evaluation. I had brought a ski jacket, a pair of gloves, boots and a scarf for him. African board members got money to buy their own winter clothes, but field staff like Chande—who came here just the once—got hand-me-downs. Most of the time, African visitors would do anything to avoid the cold, but Chande wanted to come in February.

I didn't care what Chande wanted. Once he got through customs, I would escort him downtown to the hotel, hand over his *per diem* and that would be that. Or perhaps I would dump him at reception without money for dinner. Maybe I would even walk away now, before he arrived. A week after Paulette left me, I was quick to tunnel deep into dark revenge fantasies.

The rest of the crowd strained against the rope barrier, anxiously peering through the doors whenever they opened for a glimpse of friends and family. I simply waited for passengers to make their way into the lobby past the lineup of tears, waves and laughter. I figured that—on a flight from Frankfurt—an underdressed, five-foot-nine-inch African man would stand out. For one thing, he would not be swarmed by well-wishers. There would only be me, and I hardly qualified. I was only there because a colleague—and I use the term loosely—had got me assigned to escort duty out of spite. Louise had been on my case all week after I took files from her cabinet and forgot to sign them out. When it was time to pick Chande up, she was conveniently busy. Communications staff like me, of course, always had time to take a run to the airport. The petty politics, backstabbing and poor decisions were getting to me. I had come to see that Friends of Africa was, to use one of Paulette's favourite words, dysfunctional.

As I waited for Chande to emerge, I caught a glimpse of my future that I wasn't ready to see: a man, like me, in his late-thirties, was pushing an elderly man in an airport wheelchair. A young kid—a grandson perhaps—followed behind with the baggage cart. The old man looked glum and defeated. He sat with his hands in his lap, letting the escort take control. He looked to be in his late- seventies, about the same age as my father.

Of course, my own father was in good health, but I still shuddered at the thought of his decline, and me having to care for him. He'd had his first-ever car accident last fall, about a month before my parents normally left for Florida. Despite the accident, he insisted on driving their nine-year-old station wagon all the way. I suggested a plane. I even offered to drive them down myself. He would have none of it. So I spent the next four days and nights imagining the worst scenarios: my parents killed or permanently crippled from a front-end collision, or worse, responsible for someone else's death.

I couldn't share my concerns with Paulette. She would have only agreed, steeling me to protect my father from her criticism. After six years with me, she had zero tolerance for his chauvinism, his maudlin stories about losing his best friend in the war or his careless driving. So I kept my feelings to myself, as I often did. And after four sleep-deprived nights, I snapped at her a few too many times; I was in my head a few times too often; I was emotionally absent, as she liked to say.

"I don't know who you are anymore," she'd said.

We muddled along for a few more months. I was playing Minesweeper on the computer when she announced she wanted a kitten. I refused.

"You just get attached to them, and then they die," I'd

said.

She'd stared at me as if I'd said something significant.

"When you cut yourself off from pain, you push away the potential for joy. That's what's holding you back, isn't it? That's why you're not really present. You're afraid of life."

I had no words for this accusation. I felt my face harden, my eyes narrow, my teeth clench. It was the glare, a look of hate I had promised never to inflict on her again.

After that, she stopped talking about wanting a child. I knew the end was near so I let my eyes wander, breaking an unwritten rule between us. Paulette was insecure. If I simply mentioned a woman's name from work, she got testy. A casual glance at a young woman on the canal last week finished us off. Paulette shoved my arm down and skated off in a huff. Her parting shot sounded rehearsed: "You're always looking outside of yourself for love. Maybe it's time you looked inside." I watched her disappear into the crowd. A few days later she moved out for good. I sat at home for two nights on the futon, arms folded in defeat, much like the old man in the wheelchair.

After Paulette left, I'd had vague plans to mourn before pursuing another relationship. Somehow the sight of the old man and the escort changed all that. Life was short. I didn't want to be alone any longer. It was then I saw a young woman appear in the lobby. She was about 25, blue-eyed and blond, wearing dirty, threadbare jeans, sneakers and several layers of shirts topped up with polar fleece. As she got closer, I hoped to catch her eye, but her gaze never shifted. She was either focused on getting through the airport or lost in her own world. Either way, I wanted to know her. I wanted to spend the rest of my life with her. As she passed by, I watched her park the cart in a corner beside the payphones. She unzipped a large knapsack and took out a pair of warm boots and a winter jacket.

"Excuse me," a voice said. "Are you with Friends of Africa?"

I turned to face a black man with short hair, head cocked slightly to the left.

"Mr. Chande?"

"Frank. Yes. I thought it was you. I saw the bag."

"Murray Lockhart. Welcome to Ottawa."

We shook hands, the first of many more handshakes to come. In my two years with Friends of Africa, I had noticed African men have an incessant need to touch each other. Although I was whiter than snow, I figured I would get the same treatment.

"I was expecting Louise."

"She's putting some finishing touches on your training program," I said, gritting my teeth at the lie. "She asked me to come instead."

"How kind of you."

"I'm the direct-mail coordinator. Fundraising."

"Ah," he said, and I heard judgment in his voice. No-one likes the marketers.

"You've probably seen the newsletter for donors I put out."

"No, I don't think so."

"Really? I'll have to talk to Louise about that. Let's get you into these warm clothes."

I steered him toward Knapsack Woman, but she was already gone. I tossed the bag of clothes into the chair she just vacated, and a glove tumbled onto the floor. Chande picked it up, then dug into the bag for the rest of the clothes, holding them up like Christmas presents. He was a child in a man's body, and I suddenly felt like the escort pushing the old man again. I did not want to take care of Frank Chande. As he slid on his boots, I scanned the airport in search of Knapsack Woman. No joy.

I led the way through the revolving door. As Chande emerged into the cold air, he shuddered.

"Welcome to Ottawa," I said again, this time with a bitter edge.

Chande took off a glove, reached into a snowbank and

pulled out a handful of day-old snow.

"It is so cold," he said, wiping his hand on his pants.

"Yup."

I hauled his bag into the trunk of the cab, and we set off. About halfway down the Airport Parkway, it started to snow.

"My children will never believe me. Maybe you can take a picture of me."

"No problem."

"I've been sitting so long in the plane that I really need to walk."

"Tonight? I thought you'd be dead tired."

"Not really. The first day in a new country is special. It doesn't come again. I don't expect you to come with me. I'm sure you would like to go home."

"Well, I can take your picture anyway."

"I would appreciate that."

By the time we threaded our way downtown to the hotel, it was already getting dark. While Chande took his bag to the room, I waited in the lobby, flipping through tourist brochures at the concierge desk. Chande came up from behind, all excited.

"I ran into someone in the elevator who had skates. They told me there is a large ice surface not far from here."

"They were talking about the Rideau Canal."

"Could we go there for the picture?"

It was about the last thing I wanted to do, but Chande looked so eager I couldn't refuse.

"Sure. It's not far."

When we reached the canal, it was already packed. People stood in clumps, waiting for a bench, or standing in line at the snack shacks.

"What is he doing?" Chande asked, pointing. I followed his gaze to a middle-aged man with a knapsack on his back stuffing boots onto his hands.

"Heading home. A lot of people skate to work. Some people carry their boots like that because they can't fit them into their knapsacks."

"I must have a picture of this."

"Oh," I said, trying to be delicate. "Normally, we don't take pictures of strangers here in Canada, at least not without asking."

"We have the same rule in Tanzania, but that doesn't stop the tourists there."

It was a good point. Besides, they were far enough away that the man didn't notice when Chande took a few snaps.

"Can we go down?"

"They don't like you walking on the ice. When the ice is soft, you leave footprints."

"But I see other people doing it. I would really like to walk on frozen water. It's why I wanted to come here in the winter."

He started down the steps, holding tightly onto the railing. Reluctantly, I followed. At the bottom, he stared out at the ice, which was already scratched up from the blades of countless skaters. He took a tentative step forward, and his leg shot out from under him.

"Oh my," he said, laughing nervously. He clutched the railing.

"Try shuffling along the ice rather than walking. You might find it easier."

He grabbed hold of my arm for support, and I immediately wanted to shake it off. I wanted to say, "We're in Canada. Men don't do this here." But I didn't want him to fall so we half slid, half shuffled to a bench. Sure enough a kid skated by us, his jacket open against the cold. "Look at the faggots," he called out. Chande didn't understand the taunt, or wasn't bothered by it. I was seething, wanting to lash out. But that's just what the kid wanted—a reaction—so I said nothing.

"I feel like a child learning to walk," Chande said, falling onto the bench. He handed me the camera, then got up, holding onto the bench. "Make sure you get my feet into the picture."

I snapped a few photos and sat down beside him.

"We shouldn't stay here too long. People need a place to lace their skates."

"There are other people sitting around over there," he said, pointing. "Just a few more minutes."

"All right. Sure."

"This photograph will mean a lot to my son."

"Has he always wanted to skate?"

"No, his younger brother drowned last year. John blames himself. I want to show him that water is safe, even frozen water."

I thought immediately about my father and his friend Ted, growing up in Brockville. They had been walking on the St. Lawrence River one winter. The ice gave way, and my father slipped into the hole. Ted pulled him out. The moral of the story—and with my father there was always a moral—was the importance of friendship. "The buddy system saved my life," he'd say. I'd heard this story many times. I saw myself thrashing around in that icy hole, desperately trying to survive. I could never quite picture the face of the friend who rescued me.

"The ice is pretty safe here," I said, finally.

As we sat in silence, Chande looked up the canal at a couple of teenagers passing a puck back and forth. "I see they play ice hockey here."

"They're not supposed to. They're not even supposed to have sticks on the ice."

"You have a lot of rules here that no-one seems to obey," he said, laughing.

"Yes, I guess we do."

I was ready to go, but now that I knew about his sons, I was reluctant to push Chande off the ice.

"Do you have children?" he asked.

"No. I'm not married. "

"A steady girl?"

"Until last week."

22

"That is too bad. What went wrong?"

Now he's breaking social rules, but I answer anyway.

"She wanted a child. That was a big part of it."

"And you didn't. Why not?"

Paulette had asked me the same question many times. I could never tell her the truth. I couldn't live with her rejection. But I won't see Chande again.

"It's crazy, I know, but I kept thinking a father is supposed to know things, and I don't know enough."

"I hope one day you have a child, Murray. He will teach you."

He motioned across the canal toward a woman on a bench with her knapsack, struggling to get into her skates. She stared straight at me. Her smile filled the hole in my heart.

"Go talk to her. Maybe she needs a helping hand."

This is what I thought too, but I wasn't going to try a pick-up line with Chande watching in the background.

"I'm sure she'll be fine," I said. "But it is getting late. And cold. Can you manage getting back to the hotel on your own?"

"Oh," he said, taken aback. "Yes, I think I can. Thank you so much for bringing me out here tonight."

He squeezed my arm with gratitude before letting go. I felt a twinge of guilt, but maybe Chande needed to know that frozen water was safe too, just like his son did. As he slid tentatively across the ice, I kept an eye on him, while watching the woman's progress. She was just putting her gloves on.

I heard a cry, and looked back at Chande. He was sprawled on the ice. A few people had already gathered around.

"I'm so sorry," I said, after making my way over. "I should have stayed with you."

"I'm all right," he said, rubbing his elbow. "It's not your fault. At least the ice didn't break." He smiled weakly.

I helped him to his feet, and to the other side of the canal.

"Well," he said, taking my hand.

"I can walk you back to the hotel."

"No, it's all right. I remember the way."

But he hadn't let go of my hand. Go with him, I thought. Share a confidence over a glass of wine. Ask about his sons. About his wife. About life in Tanzania, and how he gets on in the world. I was surprised this feeling passed so quickly.

I waved him off, and turned to the bench behind me. She was gone. I stared off into a sea of skaters, trying to get a fix on her. But I couldn't. There were so many knapsacks out there tonight.

Predators

Murray thumbs through the shirts in his closet, assessing his options. It's been ten years since he's been to a party with a university crowd: does he dress down or up? Paulette, of course, would know exactly what he should wear. Then again, if she hadn't left him two weeks ago, he wouldn't be going out tonight.

He looks in the mirror from different angles, making final adjustments. The pleats in his black pants and the shoulder pads in his black jacket help extend his body out farther than it really goes. He pulls the T-shirt up slightly from out of his pants, letting it ripple over his belt, accordion-style, to accentuate the bulky effect.

There's not much else he can do with the rest of his wiry body. Only 37 years old, and his hair is almost more grey than brown. He wears it long in the back these days, trying to make up for the lack up-front. If Paulette were here, she'd be on him to shave. To proclaim his independence, he leaves the bristles. The dark shadow on his face gives him an unruly look—or so he hopes.

He's ready to go, but his enthusiasm for the party, and for Stacy, has waned. He knows he's just trying to fill empty space. Nicky begat Cassandra, who begat Paulette. It's time, he thinks, to end this pattern. He makes a solemn promise not to pursue Stacy.

He met Stacy earlier in the week when she came to Friends of Africa for information about the summer internship program. Only halfway through her graduate program in international affairs at Carleton University, her head buzzed with theories and case studies. She thought her research was going to change the world. Murray had similar fantasies two years ago when he left Go Postal, the firm that handled Friends of Africa's direct-mail campaigns. He wanted to work for a cause at the source, to get away from the corporate environment, to have a meaningful life. To his surprise, he found people who worked at charities fought over cleaning the refrigerator just like everyone else.

When he had accepted Stacy's invitation, she'd written her address on the first piece of paper she saw—Paulette's final note, which he'd stupidly left on his desk. Fortunately, Stacy hadn't turned it over.

He reads Paulette's note now for the umpteenth time: "Six years is enough. I can't wait any longer. I want a child, and you're not ready. I wish it could've been you, despite everything." He flips it over again to read Stacy's address. Then he places the scrap of paper carefully in his wallet, as if it's a dance card.

Stacy's house is on Somerset Street West, about a ten-minute walk from his apartment. The melting snow from the warm spell has opened up the paths in Dundonald Park so he takes a short cut. Mistake. In the distance, he can see five teenagers on a bench with a case of beer at their feet. Unless he veers off, which is just asking for trouble, he will pass within earshot. He throws his chest out and braces for an onslaught, reviewing possible strategies: a smart remark, a withering glance, a scowl, his patented soul-destroying glare.

"Hey man, wanna buy a beer?" one of them calls out. A drunkenly jovial tone.

Murray looks straight ahead and keeps walking.

"You fuckin' deaf, or what?" the guy snaps. His friends laugh.

"Our beer not good enough for you?" another one calls out.

"What are you, a fag?" a third one yells.

"Come on back here," the first one says, shouting. "You fuckin' faggot. I'll shove this bottle up your ass." More laughter.

As Murray follows the curve of the path, it's all he can do not to run, or look behind. At any moment, he expects to hear the sound of scuffling running-shoes and clinking bottles behind him. The swoosh of air around his ears before a bottle crashes onto his head. But he passes into the street unscathed. Except for his pride.

As soon as he arrives at the party—surrounded by a sea of grad students in jeans—he feels like an old man in polyester. He spots Stacy quickly, and she waves him over.

"You're just in time. Put your beer in the cooler, then come into the living-room. Brie's going to perform."

"Brie?"

"One of my housemates."

He squeezes five bottles into the cooler and takes one with him. His hands still shake from the encounter with the teenagers. Stacy guides him into the crowded living-room. Her fingers press sensuously against his back. At least he thinks they do. No doubt, Paulette would say he's "projecting his fantasies" again. Still, he finds it comforting to let someone steer him somewhere.

"I have to sit up-front so I can see," Stacy says. "Talk to you afterwards?"

"Sure. I'll be here." She squeezes to the front, joining six or seven women on the floor. He spots an opening to the left and moves a little closer as well. About 30 of them gather in a semi-circle around a black stool that sits in front of a black backdrop.

Murray looks around, slotting people into categories: lesbians with cropped hair and nose-rings, African students, uptight white guys, scruffy lumberjacks. He watches the tall, attractive woman standing beside him for a moment. Her straight blond hair is parted in the middle and every so often, she sweeps away a strand that falls in front of her face. She wears her T-shirt loose, probably to hide tiny breasts. As the woman turns, he reads her shirt that says, "Social-work students are only in it for the Marx."

Marx sips through a straw and then brushes off a few strands of dangling hair. When she sees Murray watching her, she blows bubbles back into the glass. In response, he

27

blows across the top of the beer bottle until he gets a low note that sounds like a ship's warning signal. She turns up one corner of her mouth into a knowing, ironic smile.

As the lights dim and Brie emerges from behind the divider, the lesbians clap and whistle. A short woman, Brie stands on the stool, staring the crowd into silence. Her stomach is flat and well-toned, contrasting with her ass, which sticks up and out like the caboose of a sexy African woman. The African men grin and nudge each other.

Brie looks his way, and he smiles. Her eyes shift toward Marx. When they return to Murray, her eyes are cold, almost menacing.

"Would all those people with penises please stand back?" Brie says. "You've heard of period costumes and period films. This is period poetry. You've been warned."

Brie squats in the centre of the room, wrapping her arms around her knees and burying her head. Then she throws her arms out, stands up and shrieks. Everyone steps back now except Marx, who calmly sips her drink. She looks Murray's way, finger to her lips, in a mock shush. For the next ten minutes, Brie rants about blood clots and swollen breasts. She grabs her belly and crotch, throws her body left and right, back and forth.

"Cramps," says Marx, leaning over to Murray.

"They're obviously severe."

When the performance ends, he follows Marx into the hall, away from the speakers. Her name is Lisa, an undergraduate student in social work. They chat. With well-polished words, Murray paints a glamorous picture of Friends of Africa and its health projects. He leaves out the in-fighting and the creative accounting they use to keep administrative costs down.

"That's really terrific work," Lisa says, right on cue.

"Social work is an honourable calling, too."

"When I started the program, I felt fairly certain about it. I thought it would help me find meaningful work."

"And now?"

"I don't know. I took a few years off after high school to travel and figure out what I wanted to do. So I decided and now I'm not sure. I'm almost 30 and I've never had a real job. Pathetic, right?"

"It takes courage to admit you're not certain. You think any of these people know what they want? They're all confused. Maybe more so because they don't know they're lost."

"So you're confused too, then?"

"Big time. But see how I fooled you?"

She laughs, slurping the remains of her drink.

"I'll get you another," he says. "What are you drinking?"

"Ginger ale. On the rocks, please. Two cubes."

There's another party in the kitchen. Some new people are pressed up against the wall, including a cute young woman with short hair and dimples.

"She's taken."

He turns to face the voice behind him. It's Brie.

"I beg your pardon?"

"Lisa. Her boyfriend lives in Montreal."

"Oh, thanks, but we're just talking."

"Just thought I'd warn you. Pierre is one tough dude."

"Thanks. I can handle myself."

"You're the fellow that Stacy invited," she says. "Jerry, isn't it?"

"Murray."

"She's been talking about you non-stop all week. You work for Friends of the Earth, right?"

"Friends of Africa. But we like the Earth too."

Brie laughs, but it sounds hollow. She's baiting him.

"The ginger ale's in the side of the door," she says.

"Thanks. You're a mind reader."

How did Brie know what Lisa wanted to drink? He considers everything from hidden microphones and cameras to a lip-reading informant stationed in the hall.

"Two cubes should do it," Brie says.

"She asked for three."

He pours the ginger ale too quickly. It fizzes over the rim of the glass and onto his hand.

"Three make the drink fizz over. Something to do with physics."

"I'll remember that."

He makes his way to the living-room without looking back.

"One too many ice cubes," he says. "Sorry."

"No problem," Lisa says. "Sometimes it fizzes over the top with three. Something to do with physics."

There's a strange chemistry between Lisa and Brie. He wonders if they're lovers, but then why the line about the boyfriend?

"Have you known Brie a long time?"

"Nearly my whole life. We grew up outside of Montreal. How did you know?"

"You were the only one who didn't budge when she shrieked."

"I knew it was coming, you're right."

"Has she been out a while?"

"A year or so."

"Did you see that coming too?"

"It didn't really surprise me."

"There you are, Murray," Stacy says, calling out. Her words are slurred. "Can I steal him for a few minutes, Lisa? There's someone I want him to meet."

He's irritated, and suspects that somehow Brie has put Stacy up to this.

"Come find me later," Lisa says.

"Hey," Stacy says, pulling him close. "You're supposed to dance with the lady that brung you."

It's an expression his dad might use. It sounds strange coming from a woman in her twenties. Stacy drops her hand around his waist, and places it firmly in the small of his back. As they enter the living-room, he feels less guided than pushed. One of the lumberjacks stares at him, scowling; his chin, pockmarked from acne, is full of black stubble. Maybe he's trying for the unruly look too.

"You want me to meet that guy?"

"God no. That's Jed, my idiot brother. I want you to meet Independence over there," she says, pointing. "He's a Nigerian in my class."

"Is that a nickname?"

"A lot of Nigerians name their kids like that. But you must know that, Mr. Lockhart. You're the expert." She gives him a little push. "I'll rescue you in ten minutes."

For the next fifteen minutes, Independence rants about Canadian foreign aid policy. Murray listens—no response being required—and finally breaks away. By this time he wants the bathroom more than he wants to find Lisa. He heads upstairs, lining up behind Jed and one of his lumberjack friends. The bathroom door opens, and Lisa steps out.

"Come see me when you get out. I'm just down the hall."

"Sure."

It's just Murray and Jed now, the stubble twins, waiting in line. Jed's Harley Davidson T-shirt stinks of sweat and beer.

"I thought you were here with my sister."

"I'm not here with anybody."

"You dance with the lady that fucking brung you," he says, disappearing into the bathroom.

The expression sounds even more foreign coming out of Jed. He must have overheard Stacy complaining.

A few minutes later, Jed comes out.

"I put the seat down for you, fuckface."

Maybe it's the effect of the beers in his gut. Maybe it's the memory of the kids in the park. Whatever the reason, Murray doesn't weigh his options carefully.

In the way of all men everywhere who've had their honour tarnished, he tells Jed to fuck off.

Jed shoves Murray. Murray shoves back. Jed shoves harder, driving him against the wall.

"You asshole," Stacy says. "Get out before I throw you out."

He looks up in disbelief, but she's talking to Jed. She grabs Jed by the shoulder and nearly pushes him down the stairs. Brie watches from the banister.

"Are you all right?" Lisa says.

"Fine."

"What was all that about?"

"Nothing."

"Good thing Stacy was around to rescue you," Brie says. "Men are so unpredictable."

Murray escapes into the washroom. He lifts up the seat Jed left down for him. Stacy and Brie put Jed up to this. He needs to salvage some dignity. He will ask Lisa out, in front of Brie and Stacy. As his dad might say, he'll show them they can't keep a good man down.

He leaves the bathroom. Lisa is talking to Brie down the hall. He reads the body language. Lisa is the child, Brie is the mother. No, the big sister. Lisa shakes her head. She wants to leave, but doesn't. Brie's gravitational pull is too strong. Finally, Brie is finished. Her eyes say, "So go ahead then. You'll be sorry."

When Lisa walks over, her eyes are red and puffy.

"What's wrong?"

"Just a conflict with an old friend. Brie said you've been hitting on every woman at the party."

"She told me you've got a boyfriend in Montreal. Pierre."

"Pierre was a guy I dated twice in tenth grade. Until Brie convinced me he wasn't good enough."

They smile at each other ruefully, connected by Brie's deceit. He writes down Lisa's number on his dance card, just below Stacy's address. She recites it loudly to make sure Brie and Stacy hear. She even moves slightly to give them a better view of the transaction. They're using each other. No matter.

Sleepover

After we made love, Lisa and I lay in my bed with the lights out, staring at the glow-in-the-dark planets on the ceiling. Paulette had arranged this miniature galaxy. She knew I loved astronomy, but she wanted to spur my interest in astrology. It didn't work. As I dithered over having children, and we lapsed more often into helpless silence, she would often lie there, trying to find answers in the stars.

"What are those three stars in a row?" Lisa said.

"It's the belt of Orion, the hunter. That's his sword hanging down below."

"It doesn't look like a sword."

"You have to use your imagination."

She fell silent. Was she imagining Brie? Wishing she was in her friend's arms instead? I couldn't bear to think it.

"This was so totally unexpected," she said. "It's been a while for me. I hope we didn't make a mistake."

"Is that what you think?"

"I don't know."

We lay in silence until she fell asleep. I turned on my side, listening to her steady breathing, watching her nose twitch from the stray hairs that tickled her face, pulling the duvet over her bare shoulder to keep her warm. She purred softly.

I turned on my back again to stare at the stars. The two weeks of bachelorhood that followed six years with Paulette felt like a long time for me too. Tomorrow afternoon, I would shovel snow off the cottage roof. I wanted Lisa to come with me. Not to help, just for company. Just to watch. But I was afraid she would say no. The milky way offered no guidance.

Last night, on our second date, she wanted to know what shaped me. Wound bonding, Paulette used to call it. I knew the routine: the more traumatic the incident, the better.

"I didn't get touched much as a child. That's why I crave it

33

now."

"Ditto."

"I watched a lot of TV. I could recite commercials. That's why I ended up in fundraising, I think."

"Come on, Murray. Tell me something meaningful."

"I'm compulsive. I play a lot of computer games."

"Deeper."

"I went home once, about fifteen years ago, with my ear pierced. It traumatized my father. I think it unleashed pent-up feelings of loss about his best friend who'd been killed in World War II. He never talked about Ted until then, and now he doesn't stop."

"What's the connection between Ted and the earring?"

"I guess he lost Ted, and then he thought he'd lost me to the world of homosexuals."

"Too weird."

She'd felt my ear lobes.

"I can't find the hole."

"I let it grow over."

"Out of love for your dad? That's very noble."

"I consider it a moment of weakness. I've been told I let him run my life. He's got this phone shtick. They get a better deal on long distance in Florida. So he rings once, to see if I'm home, and then hangs up. Then I call him back and hang up. Then he calls me back. He doesn't want to get caught by the voicemail."

"It sounds very sweet."

Paulette didn't think so. She called me a wimp, once, for going along with my dad's system. I had no words for her. I unleashed the glare—a devastating look of hate and disdain. She never really trusted me again.

"Tell me about your hopes and dreams," Lisa had said.

"*My Dinner with Andre* is my favourite film. Andre goes to Findhorn, a spiritual community in Scotland. He looks at a leaf and sees the veins growing inside. He runs through the woods feeling alive for the first time in his life. I would love

34

to find that forest."

"What's holding you back?"

"What do you mean?"

"Your greatest hope is your greatest fear. Part of us is afraid to get what we want."

"I don't think I have a fear around the forest."

"But you haven't tried to find it. Maybe you don't know what your fear is yet."

She sounded much wiser than her 25 years. Twelve years older, I was not nearly as evolved. Maybe that's why Lisa wondered if we'd made a mistake.

As we'd sat and talked, I had touched her hand, tracing a finger down the veins in her palm. She stuck out her other hand.

"Do you do feet, too?"

"My specialty."

She started to strip out of her socks.

"No, it's better with socks on first. Then take them off and I'll do it again."

We took turns, alternating feet. She gave as good as she got. Her light strokes tickled so deliciously I gripped the sides of the bed.

Cassandra had got bored of my feet. Paulette had refused to go near them. Nicky tried, but she wanted to massage them. All the other girlfriends never lasted long enough to reach this stage. Yet here I was with Lisa, foot stroking on our second date. We turned off the light and stripped off the rest of our clothes. I didn't need to find Andre's forest: I felt alive with her.

Where had she learned to give and receive so? From Brie? Was that why I threatened Brie so much? I had vanquished her at the party, but she had a deep hold on Lisa that I needed to understand. In between touching, I steered conversation toward Lisa's childhood.

"I told you how my dad drank," Lisa had said. "When he

35

died in the car accident, my sister started drinking, and my mom started sleeping around. I couldn't handle it so I spent a lot of time at Brie's house."

"She supported you."

"I was good for her too. Her brother was a creep. He would lock her in the closet for hours when their parents were out. I had a sleepover there once, and I passed his bedroom. He was standing there in the open doorway, naked, fondling himself."

"You think there was some abuse?"

"I don't know. Why are you so interested?"

"Keep your friends close, your enemies closer."

"I don't like the way you're talking about her. She's my best bud, Murray."

"Sorry."

I wanted to be Lisa's best bud. She sensed it too. We had made love because we were naked from all of our touching. It was an afterthought. Maybe that's why she wondered if we'd made a mistake.

In mid-morning, I left Lisa curled in fetal position, and half eased, half tumbled my way off the mattress. As my left hand touched the floor, I landed on last night's condom. I lay on my stomach, inspecting the tiny sac. There wasn't much in it. Either the remnants had spilled onto the floor or inside Lisa. Or maybe this is all there was. I slipped out of the bedroom. I needed space.

The phone rang once. I hesitated. Not calling Dad back was a protest, a tiny attempt to wave the Murray Lockhart flag of independence. But I wanted to get the call over before Lisa woke up.

"We heard about the storm," Dad said. "I don't want to leave the roof too long with all that snow."

"It's mostly melted, but I'm going out there today."

"I don't know why you can't get someone else to do it," Mom said, from the other extension.

"He'll use the safety belt. You don't want someone else up there. What if they fall and break their neck? We don't have liability insurance. They could take us for all we've got."

"So you'd rather have your son break his neck?"

"I'm not going to break my neck, Mom!"

"We don't even know for sure if it is our cottage, until you get the surveyor in," she said.

"What the hell are you talking about? Of course it's our cottage. All I said was there might be a problem with the deed."

"Well, I don't understand why you can't leave snow on the roof. You go through this every year, and nothing has ever happened."

"Nothing happens because we shovel the snow off."

"Well maybe Murray should take a friend with him. You know, the buddy system. Do you have a friend who could go with you?"

"I'll be fine."

"He's not going skating on the river, for god's sake."

"Make sure you wear the safety belt."

"Your mother's right about that. It's slippery up there. Easy to make a mistake."

I hung up just as I heard stirring from the bedroom. A few moments later, Lisa appeared, fully dressed. She seemed flustered.

"Have a shower if you want."

"I've got to get going. I'm helping a friend and then I have to finish an essay. It's due Monday."

"Oh."

I was certain Brie was the friend. I saw myself on a windy roof, shovelling snow, alone, for the rest of my days.

"I should have got you up sooner."

"It's all right. It's not like we planned last night."

I hugged her, but she felt standoffish. She was slipping away.

"So you think we made a mistake?" I said.

"No."

But it was my turn now to wonder.

Lisa lived in a bachelor apartment on the other side of Bronson Avenue, a beer bottle's toss from the drug dealers on Bell Street. Although she had survived this long without me, I liked to think I was protecting her.

It was unusually mild for late February, the kind of day when melting snow drained into sewers, and the universe seemed to be unfolding as it should. We opened the necks of our jackets and took off our gloves, and after a while, I took her hand. It felt sweaty, not dry like last night. On the other side of Lyon Street, an older woman headed in our direction, overdressed for the weather and muttering to herself. Abruptly, she turned and walked back the way she came.

"She looks confused," Lisa said. "Maybe she's lost."

"I don't think she's going anywhere in particular. She's just going."

Lisa watched the woman for a few more moments. "Whenever I see a bag lady, I think of my sister. I worry she'll end up on the street."

"My dad used to talk about 'ending up in the poor house.' I grew up thinking it was a real place where people were sent when they lost their money. I kept worrying it would happen to us."

"God, that's awful."

"I suppose. But you grow up. You get over it."

"Sometimes you do."

I squeezed her hand. She squeezed back. We were frayed wires, shorting out and re-connecting at random.

When we reached her apartment, we could hear music from behind the door.

"Did you leave the stereo on?"

"I can't remember."

"I'll wait here until you open the door."

"It's okay. If someone had broken in, they wouldn't be sitting around listening to Ani DiFranco."

"All the same."

Lisa flung a strand of hair behind her ear as she fumbled with the key. She opened the door and at the end of the short entranceway, I saw Brie flaked out on Lisa's beanbag chair. She squeezed her butt more firmly into the beans. The motion said, "You have entered my sphere of influence. I've got the key. I belong here. You are the intruder." I saw all this in a second, and Brie knew it.

"You're blushing. That can only mean one thing. The big bang."

"Brie!" Lisa squealed with nervous, embarrassed laughter. She slipped off her boots and coat. I stood there, sweating in my winter jacket.

"I guess we'll be seeing more of you, Murray. We'll have to sit down over coffee. I can tell you some stories."

"Thanks. I'll wait for the movie."

"X-rated."

"I'll bring toilet paper."

Brie actually laughed.

"I'm beginning to like you, Murray. Too bad you can't stay."

I didn't respond. She had me. We both knew it.

"Will you give us a moment? Lisa said.

"I'll wait for you right here. I forgot my jammies, by the way. We'll have to do it like the old days. Camping in the backyard under the stars."

Lisa took me back into the foyer outside her apartment for privacy.

"Star-crossed lovers," I said. She laughed.

"You're very understanding. You get extra points for that."

"Is this a contest?"

She blushed again. I held on to one of her hands and stroked it lightly, but my touch was fused with anxiety and desperation. She was distracted. The force of Brie's presence in the other room was pulling her. It made me want to pull back.

"You're sure you don't want to watch me shovel snow instead?" I laughed, pretending it was a joke.

"I wish I could. I really do. You'll be okay on your own?"

"There's a safety belt."

"Does it come with a sword?"

"You have to imagine it."

The in-jokes about Paulette's constellations on my ceiling was all it took to bring us back to my bed. Her eyes confirmed it: last night was not a mistake for her. We would soon push Brie out of our orbit.

I wouldn't wear the belt this year. Desire for Lisa would hold me firm. I would stand on the roof, one foot on either side of the peak, sword raised over my head, and proclaim to the heavens that my hunt for the perfect woman was over. This time I would mean it.

Channel Markers

About halfway to his parents' cottage near Brockville, Murray tells Lisa they're in limbo. "The American stations are just getting stronger the closer we get to the border," he says.

"Here's something," Lisa says. A deep male voice crackles, ending his patter just before the first chords of Boston's "More Than a Feeling."

"American," he says, turning it off.

"What does it matter?"

"It just does."

Lisa slips the tape of the Indigo Girls into the deck again, but they're as warbly as ever. He punches the eject button, shooting the tape under his feet.

"You'd think Brie would get a CD player," he says.

"Why don't you buy her one? A gift for lending us the car again."

"This is no favour. It's just another way for her to control us."

"You're paranoid."

"That doesn't mean I'm wrong. You told me she's tried to sabotage all your relationships. Her mission in life is to come between us. For the past three months, she's just tried to get under my skin."

"She's obviously doing a good job."

He clams up, hands clenched at ten and two. Lisa rolls down the window and sticks her hand out, holding it up against the wind. The common armrest stays vacant, a no man's land. They're alone, but when he checks his mirror, he can almost see Brie on the back seat, devising new ways to poison their relationship: "I'm going to win, Murray. It's just a matter of time until Lisa comes out, and comes home."

"We have a special bond," Lisa says. "We helped each other get through our childhood and adolescence. If you had a really old friend in your life, you'd understand. From what you've said about your dad and his friend Ted, I bet he'd understand."

"Ted isn't a friend. He's a ghost. He's an obsession. If that's what it means to have an old friend, I'll pass."

"It must have been hard for you."

"What?"

"Growing up in Ted's shadow."

"I told you. He hardly ever talked about the war until I came home that time with the earring. Then he thought I was gay, and somehow that brought everything back. Before that, Ted wasn't an issue. I didn't grow up in his shadow."

"The shadow was still there. You just didn't see it. But you obviously felt it."

"I've had enough Ted and Brie. Let's go over the rules again."

She sighs.

"If it's yellow let it mellow, if it's brown flush it down," he says.

"That's so disgusting. I can't stand the smell of urine."

"If you've just got urine on the toilet paper, don't flush it. Put it in the waste paper basket."

"You never told me that."

"It's a septic system. My parents are very particular. They don't want to call the honeydippers."

"The what?"

"Honeydippers are the guys who clean septic tanks."

"I'm just starting my period. Are tampons okay to flush down?"

"Jesus, Lisa."

"Gotcha."

She pokes him gently in the side and he bursts into a fit of nervous laughter.

"And remember to call them Mr. and Mrs. Lockhart. They're old school."

"Your Mom will insist I call them Burt and Virgie. I

remember. I think you're the one who needs a honeydipper."

Murray is thirteen years old, leaning on a shovel, watching his father pace over the grass below the bathroom window. Burt's footsteps squish the little mounds of earth that the moles have pushed above the surface. Every so often, he stops to examine the map clenched in his hands.

"I'd say it's about here."

He hands Murray the map and takes the shovel.

"I think it was more to the left," says his mother, poking her head out of the bathroom window.

Burt shakes his head with a dismissive snort.

"I've got the map, Virgie."

"Well I drew it twenty years ago."

"That's why I'm having trouble finding the damn thing now."

"Well you'd better hurry up. The honeydipper is coming soon."

"Then let me get at it for Christ's sake."

The window snaps shut.

It's early yet and the thick grass is still wet with dew. Murray's running shoes are almost soaked. He stands on a boulder in the rock garden, watching sweat pour off his father's face.

"Want some help?" Murray says.

"No," Burt says, puffing. "I can manage."

Murray wishes his father would trust him to do it right, but then again, he's happy enough to be watching. Besides, his father likes an audience.

"Pay attention. One day you'll have to do this."

Murray keeps track of the piles of dug-up earth on the ground. When his time comes, many years from now, he'll know how many shovelfuls it takes.

On the twenty-third scoop, Burt hits metal. Most of the tank is still buried to the left, just like Virginia said. It takes him another half hour to clear off the surface, which is five feet across. He kneels down and unlatches the top.

"Stand back. It's going to be sweet."

"I'll be all right."

"Suit yourself."

As the wave of stench rises, Murray keeps his face neutral to show he can take it, but his body shudders with revulsion. He steps back.

"I warned you."

In his father's voice, Murray can hear both triumph and disappointment.

"What are you thinking about?"

"Nothing."

"You shuddered."

"No I didn't."

"Okay, Murray. Are we there yet?" she says, putting on a child-like whine.

"Almost."

Murray takes the scenic route along Highway 2, pointing out the landmarks on the east side of Brockville—the mini-putt course, the asylum, the mansions.

"All these houses are right on the lake," she says.

"River."

"Whatever."

They drive in silence until they reach the road into Pine Tree Point. Over the ridge, the river comes back into view.

"Look, there's a boat."

"A Laker. If you're lucky, you'll see two ships pass each other. From up here, it'll look like they'll crash."

Lisa is intrigued that all the cottages have names like "High Point" and "Country Home" carved into rustic sign posts or mounted above the front door.

"What's the name of your cottage?"

"We don't have one. We've always just called it 'the cottage.'"

"Why not name it?"

"We've never felt the need." He pauses for effect. "Maybe it's because we know who we are."

"I'm happy for you."

They pass a newcomer chopping wood on his back-lot. There's an arrogance about these people, the way they tear down cottages and put up permanent homes, how their docks extend farther into the river than anyone else's. The fellow leans on his axe, watching as the car passes. Murray wants to shout, "What are you looking at? You're the stranger here."

As they approach the cottage, Murray points to the dark patch of oil in the road that extends about twenty feet on either side of the property. "That there's the sign we're heading into Lockhart territory," he says, putting on his best western drawl. "My pa oils the road to keep the dust down."

"I'm sure that's good for the soil."

"What's good for Burt Lockhart is what counts."

After they park and haul their bags across the oily road, Murray spots the neighbour's dog, a Golden Retriever.

"Don't even think about it, Sadie," he says, shooing her away. "If Burt sees you dumping a load on the lawn, he'll get out his pellet gun."

"You're kidding."

"Burt's not fond of strays."

"He's not a stray. He's a pet."

"If he's not leashed, he's a stray."

They continue walking through the long grass, past the garden and the apple tree.

"What's the point of having a cottage if you have to mow the lawn?"

"I asked the same question when I was a kid. I hated that job. Especially since Dad would always hold the cord for me. He still does."

"Why don't you tell him to stop?"

"I do."

He can almost hear her fingers flipping through her self-help books, searching for him in one of the case studies.

45

She points to the American and Canadian flags flapping side by side.

"It's a good thing you know who you are," she says. "Someone less secure might get confused."

"When I inherit the cottage, the Stars and Stripes come down."

"Have you told him that?"

"There's no telling him anything."

She points across the river. "Does that island have a name? Or do you just call it 'the island?'"

"That, my dear, is the U.S. of A."

"No kidding."

"There's my mom," he says, pointing to the east side of the cottage. Her eyesight is getting worse. As she moves the watering bucket back and forth across the petunia bed, the new bifocals hanging around her neck bounce gently against her cardigan. She waves, walking toward the cottage to wait for them. She steps up on the porch stairs to stay on the same level as Lisa. They appraise each other.

"Where's Dad?"

"Fixing the pump. It's acting up again. I'm afraid we can't flush the toilet."

"We can always go in the woods," Lisa says, winking behind Virginia's back.

"Mr. Lockhart will get it fixed," Virginia says, coldly.

Lisa glances at Murray, mouthing "What did I say?" to him.

Once inside, Lisa follows Murray's advice, asking about the decor, the plants and the garden.

"You have a lovely cabin, Mrs. Lockhart."

"Thank you. I just have to finish cleaning up the kitchen."

There is no invitation to call her "Virgie," and Lisa looks to Murray for help.

"Cottage," he says, "not cabin."

Murray follows Lisa to the kitchen. His mother is wiping the plates down with toilet paper before putting them in the dishwasher. Lisa looks at him, mouthing: "This is insane!"

As Virginia readies the chicken breasts, Lisa puts a package of tofu burgers from her bag on the counter.

"You don't like chicken?"

"I'm a vegetarian."

"Oh."

As Virginia turns to get a knife, Lisa pulls Murray into the dining-room.

"Thanks a lot. Why didn't you tell her?"

"I didn't think you'd have the gall to bring your own food. I thought you'd just put the chicken to one side."

"She hates me."

"She doesn't know you."

"When she knows me, she'll really hate me."

They walk around the cottage. Along the west side, she stops at the television aerial, touching the faded numbers painted on different points of the pole.

"13, 4, 11," she reads. "What's this?"

"It helps with the tuning. Those are the Ottawa and Kingston channels."

"No cable, I guess."

"We didn't need it. CBS and NBC come in clear enough without it. Better than the Canadian stations, in fact. That's why they're not marked on the pole."

"Those damned Americans, eh, Murray? Always taking over the airwaves."

He gives her a paternal look. Patient, but not condescending, as if she doesn't yet understand the world.

"Come on, I'll show you my dad."

They walk to the edge of the cliff and peer over.

"See that big tree that comes up from the river? See the wooden platform? Now, if you look closely, you'll see the roof of the pumphouse tucked underneath the cliff."

"Got it. I see his back."

Burt stands up on the wooden platform. He's six-five, but

47

from up here, Murray can see he's starting to stoop. He puts a screwdriver and a monkey-wrench into his tool-belt. As his father grabs the limb of the tree to swing himself off the platform, Murray holds his breath.

"Oh my god," Lisa says, clutching his arm. "If he slipped, he would have fallen into the river. He could have cracked his skull."

"He's done that a thousand times. He knows what he's doing."

Burt disappears under the veil of the cliff.

"So you think he's got the pump fixed?"

"He's brought his tools up. That means the job's done."

"Are you good with tools too?"

"I spent most of my time trying to get out of work. Or else I would just hand him tools and watch. He likes to do things himself. We'll have a session one of these days. He'll show me the ropes."

"He's almost 80. I wouldn't wait much longer."

"He's fine. You saw him. He'll live to be a hundred."

While they wait for Burt, he points out the shoal in front of their cottage. She gazes at the two flags flying near the cliff, then looks at the speedboats bouncing over choppy waves in the channel.

"What are those white things?"

"Channel markers. The ships have to pass between them."

"So where's the border?"

"More or less in the middle of the river."

"And what if boats cross over?"

"No big deal. Boats come and go as they please."

"Those Americans, eh? First they take over the airwaves, then they take over the waves."

"Joke all you want. I spent my whole life listening to my dad talk about Americans. They stand up for what they believe in. They've got balls. Backbone. Guts. They're the best. When something big happened in Canada, we'd watch to see if we'd made the American news. Then we'd know it had really happened."

He stops, breathless, heart beating.

"I think you should name your cottage."

Burt emerges and, unaware of them, walks straight to the garage. His mother opens the screendoor on the patio and looks around.

"I thought I saw your father come up."

"He went that-a-way," says Lisa, pointing.

"Can you tell him it's time to light the barbecue?"

"We can light it," says Lisa.

"No, Mr. Lockhart will do it."

Virginia returns to the kitchen.

"Now she thinks I'm going to break her barbecue."

"It's not that. Dad likes to do it."

"It's a barbecue."

"Trust me on this."

Burt wears the tool-belt slung low on the waist. He walks toward them, slightly bent over, the rubber handle of the hammer bouncing lightly against his thigh.

"He looks like a gunslinger," Lisa says.

"Damned pump wouldn't prime," Burt says. "But I got her goin'."

"Dad, this is Lisa."

"Hello Mr. Lockhart."

"Call me Burt. I won't shake hands with you. I've got to wash up first."

"Mom wants you to light the barbecue."

"We can do it for you," Lisa says.

"No that's all right. It's fiddly."

He spins around quickly, and loses his balance for a second before going inside the cottage.

"Great. I call him Burt, and I call your mother Mrs. Lockhart."

A few minutes later, Burt is back to fire up the gas barbecue. He's forgotten about Lisa until he sees the tofu burgers sitting on the plate.

"What's this?"

"Lisa's a vegetarian."

"You're always dating girls who eat rabbit food."

She glares at Murray.

"Come here," Burt says, taking her hand. "I want to show you something."

"Gladly."

He steers her inside, toward the mantelpiece. Murray follows.

"There's Ted," he says, pointing to a picture. "We grew up together and then, through some miracle, ended up on the same aircraft carrier during the war—*HMS Nabob*."

"Burt," Virginia calls out. "Put the chicken on and those other things."

"We were attacking the *Tirpitz* when they got him." He pauses to wipe his eyes. "He was caught below deck when the torpedo hit. I tried to reach him, but there was so much chaos."

"I'm sorry to hear that."

"Burt!"

"You don't have to shout. I'm not deaf."

"Lisa doesn't want to hear all those old stories."

Lisa looks over at Murray, mouthing: "She's taking my side!"

As they settle down at the table for lunch, Burt picks up where he left off.

"Ted and I grew up on the river. We were best friends."

"That was a long time ago," Virginia says, cutting him off.

Burt picks away at his food.

"Look," Lisa says, pointing out the window. "A little boat is pulling another boat."

"A tugboat is towing a barge," Murray says. "She's a real landlubber, eh Dad?"

"None of your girlfriends ever know anything about the river."

"The grass is getting long," Lisa says, glaring at Murray. "Your loving son was hoping to cut it for you after lunch."

"Well that would be a help. I'll give you a hand."

"I can manage it, Dad."

"Well, let me set you up."

"He can cut the lawn without you," Virginia says.

"It's tricky with that mower. It's easier if I hold the cord out of the way."

"Dad, the whole point is for me to help you. If you're going to follow me around, then you're not getting a break."

"All right. But let me get it out for you."

"Can I help you with the clean-up, Mrs. Lockhart?"

"I'll just stack them. And call me Virgie."

Lisa gives Murray a thumbs-up as he's heading out the door with Burt.

When Burt opens the garage door, Sadie bounds out of the bushes.

"That damned dog," Burt says. "Always crapping on the lawn. One of these days, I'm going to dump it on their lawn and see how they like it."

"That's not going to help things."

"You sound just like your mother."

Burt picks a fallen apple off the ground and flings it close to the dog.

"Get out of here. Get!"

Sadie runs after the apple. She picks it up in her mouth, spitting it out when she realizes it's not a ball. Burt rolls the lawnmower out of the garage, uncoiling the long extension cord. Sadie watches until Murray throws the switch.

When Murray reaches the end of one row and flips the handle over, the cord gets tangled in his feet. He's heading toward Burt now. Every few feet he stops and flicks the cord out of harm's way. At the end of his second pass, as he flips the handle again, he feels tension in the cord. Burt is walking alongside, feeding him slack.

51

He puts up with it, like he always does, telling himself that Burt needs to do it. But then Lisa appears. She walks toward him, and he stops.

"What?"

"You missed a spot."

She points to a patch under the apple tree.

"I haven't gone there yet."

"Just thought I'd tell you."

"You sound like Brie."

"What's the hold-up?" Burt says.

"Nothing."

Lisa sits on the stone porch, opens her journal and begins to write down all her mental notes. A few moments later, as he turns the corner, Lisa is out of sight again. He focuses on the river side to avoid passing her. Burt is just following his lead, trying not to get the cord tangled around the trees. But then they run out of line, and the plug gets pulled from the socket. The lawnmower dies without a sputter of protest.

"Hang on," Burt says. "I'll plug it in at the front."

Burt starts pulling the extension cord across the grass. Murray walks toward the cliff and stares at the river. The wind is picking up a little as it often does in the afternoon.

Behind him, the mower's engine kicks in again, and Burt stands with cord in his hand. He seems impatient.

"It's okay," Murray says, calling out over the noise. "I can manage."

He starts to push the mower, but still feels Burt holding the cord.

Murray nods at him again. "I can do it! It's okay!"

"Is something wrong?" Burt yells.

Murray stops the machine and walks back toward him.

"I can do this on my own. You don't have to follow me."

"I don't mind. It's very easy to run over the cord. I do it all the time."

Murray spots Lisa coming around.

"Will you let me do it?" His voice has an edge now.

"Fine," he says, throwing the cord on the ground. He turns away quickly, toward the front of the cottage. As he disappears, Lisa starts walking toward Murray. But then they hear Burt cry out, and they rush to the front of the yard.

Burt is squatting on one knee in the long grass under the apple tree.

Murray runs up to him first.

"Are you all right?"

"It's that damned dog." Burt is up on his feet, scraping his shoe against the grass.

"What happened?" It's Virginia at the front door.

"That dog," Burt says, pointing at his shoe. "One day I'm going to shoot that animal."

"You'll do no such thing," Virginia says, arms wrapped tightly across her chest.

"To hell with it," Burt says, voice shaking. "Let's see how they like it."

He marches off to the garage, returning with a shovel.

Virginia retreats inside the cottage, shutting the door hard behind her. Lisa and Murray stand there together, watching Burt make his way down the road. Behind them, the flags start to flutter in the growing breeze.

"It's been a long time coming," Murray says.

"You don't think this is about the dog? He's just trying to save face. He just wanted to help you with the lawnmower. Why is it men can't accept help?"

That was my declaration of independence, he wants to say. *And I only hurt my dad because I didn't want to appear weak in front of you. Now, somehow, refusing his help has made me appear even weaker? I don't get it.*

She walks to the patch of grass that's been pummelled by the shovel.

"God it still stinks. Oh. That's why. He missed a spot. Maybe you should call him back so he can get this bit too."

Murray squats in front of the faeces, breathing in deeply.

"I don't smell a thing."

Off-Season

I keep expecting someone to walk along the beach in one of my shirts. It's mid-September, off-season in Tanzania. The hotel restaurant is nearly empty. From the patio, two security guards make the rounds, rifles slung casually over their shoulders. They walk on the firm sand a few feet above the waterline, watching the trawlers, the surf, everything but what they're supposed to watch. Someone is probably emptying my closet right now.

Frank Chande, the field officer for Friends of Africa in Tanzania, arranged this end-of-mission vacation. When Frank was in Ottawa last February, walking tentatively on the Rideau Canal, he had been the child. Here, on his own turf, he was the parent, prone to unsolicited health-and-security advice. "Wash your hands," he told me. "If someone steals from you, don't chase them. You never know what awaits you down some blind alley."

I brush my foot against the knapsack under the table, stuffed with my camera. Still there. They can only get my clothes now. In through the balcony door that won't lock and out through the front door, which the chambermaid probably left wide open.

Frank has got to me. Part of me buys his paternal advice, another part rejects it. When he warned me about the ladies of ill repute and their tough pimps, it sounded like the "keep your pecker in your pants" advice I got from my father when I left for university. But sure enough, the night before we left for Talime in the north, I heard a tap on my hotel-room door, and then a sexy woman's voice that said, "Love is passing you by." I kept the door shut and locked, but part of me wanted to break out and ravish her, just so I could hang the ripped panties around Frank's rear-view mirror the next morning.

I would settle now for the memory of an affair with Rhobi Juma, the executive director of Whole Women, an organization fighting against female genital mutilation. I felt the attraction as soon as Frank and I walked into her office in Talime. She was at her desk, sitting behind a 386 computer, talking intensely on the telephone in Swahili and scribbling a message on a notepad with her free hand. When she saw us, her face changed from consternation to sheer delight. She stood up, slender and tall, and smoothed out her skirt. Her eyes were so vibrant, so alive, so flirtatious. She was about 40 years old. I checked her hand: no wedding ring.

We sat around a small table in her office.

"It's a good time to visit us. We're just getting ready for FGM season. Next month, we would be too busy."

"FGM season?"

"Frank, you haven't told Murray about this?" She pushed Frank's hand on the table. Frank grinned, and shook his head like a shy schoolboy.

"In December, they round up the girls like chickens, and take them to the hills and mountains to be cut," she said. "It's illegal so they do it now in secret. Our job is to educate the mutilators about the health impact on the girls, and to get the elders in the village to protect them."

"They are preparing a proposal for a new project now called 'Circumcision through Words,'" Frank said. "They do this in Kenya. It's a coming-of-age ritual for girls where they can become women without being mutilated."

"The ritual is important, but we also want to start an income-generating project for mutilators," Rhobi said. "Because FGM isn't just about culture and tradition—it's also about poverty. The mutilators are afraid they will lose their income."

"And I have explained how this is outside of our mandate," Frank said, smiling.

"It is a friendly disagreement," Rhobi said, smiling back. "I am still planning to change Frank's mind."

The words felt loaded, and when the two of them shared another glance, I understood. The flirtatious looks were directed at Frank, not me. Later, in the Land Rover heading back to Dar es Salaam, I kept asking about Rhobi, as if this would bring me closer. She had been mutilated as a young girl and lost her sister to blood poisoning caused by FGM. When she'd protected her own daughter, her husband had disowned her. She had built up Whole Women from scratch.

"Do you think we will fund this project for the mutilators?"

"I'm sure we can find a way."

"That's what she seemed to think."

Frank laughed. "She has strong powers of persuasion."

"I think she likes you."

"Hang on!" he said. As he swerved, my head bumped against the hand grip. The wheels, skidding against the unpaved shoulder, stirred up dust, which seeped through the floor panels.

"Sorry," he said, pulling back onto the road. "That car came straight at us."

I coughed from the dust in my throat. "Didn't he see us?"

"He wanted me to move for him."

"That's crazy."

"Yes. You never know what people will do. All you can do is be alert, and not take foolish risks." He threw me a meaningful look.

I recognized the signs of an inner struggle, which, so far, Frank was winning. I admired his self-discipline, his commitment, his politics, his fear of AIDS—whatever it was that kept him true to Halima, his wife. It did nothing for me, however. I still wondered whether, after Lisa and I moved in together in October, my restless eyes would cease their wandering. I took a silent pledge to follow Frank's example: enjoy the flirtation, but know when to stop. And then I put Rhobi out of my thoughts. It worked for a while. The bustle of the trip kept me preoccupied. It's only now, a week later, in the stillness of this vacant hotel, that I feel the pain of her absence. Why don't I miss Lisa? I don't know.

The rum-and-Coke finally arrives on the rocks, just like last night. I chase the ice cubes around with a spoon, splashing drink everywhere. Finally, I leave the cubes to float, letting any bacteria from the water merge with the drink. Live dangerously.

A young white woman enters the restaurant from the patio. She's wearing a broad sunhat, a wrap skirt and open-toed sandals, and carrying a sweater over one arm. There's no-one else in the restaurant, but she doesn't look up. Instead, she takes off her sunglasses and hat, and pretends to read a paperback—or so it seems. I feel a pang of longing, a desire to win her over.

The universe is throwing out a challenge: fall prey to my baser instincts or invoke the spirit of Frank Chande. I choose to fight. I pull postcards from my knapsack to keep busy. Fishing trawlers for my parents. The bare-breasted African woman for Lisa. I want to show that I trust she won't turn into a lesbian while I'm away.

For inspiration, I take out a picture from the money-belt strapped to my chest. Lisa and I had found an old photo booth in a shopping centre and celebrated our three-month anniversary with a few poses. I had really wanted this to be romantic, but Lisa wasn't into it. Eyes crossed, tongue out. Even in this one, the only straight pose, she played to the camera. Her eyes were mock serious while I looked straight ahead, lips in a tight smile.

When the customs officer at the airport in Dar es Salaam went through my wallet, and found the photo, he had smiled, flashing impossibly white teeth.

"Your wife?"

Not exactly, sir. We may marry one day, but for now, we're just testing the waters. The truth is, we're going to live together because I'm afraid of losing Lisa to her lesbian best friend, Brie. She's going to live with me, I think, because it makes sense economically, and maybe because she wants some distance from Brie. Lisa and I are fond of each other. Maybe it's love, I'm not sure.

"Yes," I'd said. "My wife."

Keep it simple. A wrong answer, even if it's the truth, can create problems. You never know what they want to hear so you look for clues, like smiles. I had smiled back—the proud husband—and the man's smile had grown deeper. He had handed back the photo, his dirty thumbprint on our faces an official stamp of approval. For him, a relationship was probably home-cooked meals, sex on-demand and a room full of poor, but happy children. For me, it was take-out food, analytical sex and the fear of creating another generation of dysfunctional kids.

The meal arrives so I put the photo away, and stack the postcard with the others. The fish is tasty enough, but the vegetables are overcooked. The woman gets served too and finally makes eye contact. She smiles, and my fragile resolve melts. I lift my glass slightly in greeting. When she returns the gesture, I get a rush, but it's not enough. So I rip a page from my travel journal and write:

> Since the main course leaves something to be desired, perhaps you would care to join me for dessert? It may not affect the food, but your company would improve the ambience considerably!

I signal to the waiter, and put the message on the tray, along with a shilling for a tip. I nod in the direction of the woman. The waiter understands suave. He takes it over, no questions asked. My knee vibrates under the table as the woman reads the note. I lean into my foot, planting it firmly on the floor. She looks up, smiles, picks up her things and walks to my table.

Her name is Greta, a tourist from Germany. She tried to visit Zanzibar for a few days, but couldn't get a ferry and ended up at this beach hotel for the night. Like me, she's leaving tomorrow. Greta is about my age. Her eyes search my face, checking me out. After a few moments, she seems to relax. She applies lip balm slowly to her bottom lip, a gesture I find erotic.

"Too much sun today," she says.

"What, with that big hat?" I say, touching the rim. She laughs.

As the sun sets, we exchange tales over coffee and crème caramel. My carefully orchestrated trip to visit projects is no match for her stories of broken-down buses and hobnobbing with the locals. Still, she's impressed, as most are, that I work for a group like Friends of Africa.

When the mosquitoes come out, she pulls on the sweater to protect her bare arms.

"I'm not taking any pills," she says. "You?"

"Yes, but I went to the north. I wanted to be careful, although they say malaria is just as bad in Dar as it is up-country." I throw my head back over my left shoulder. For all I know, I'm pointing toward the men's room.

"I was afraid of the side-effects," she says. "They said it can make you paranoid."

"They're always saying that. You can't trust 'em."

She laughs.

"Did you get a mosquito net in your room?" I say.

"No. You?"

"It took me an hour to untangle it. It's full of holes any-way."

"Better than nothing," Greta says, laughing. "Can I see your postcards?" She flips through them, smiling at the roaring lions. "It's hard to find something unusual, isn't it?" She pauses next at the bare-chested woman, and mentions seeing two young African girls take off their tops on a beach in Dar. "They were about fourteen. The only people who watched them were the whites."

She flashes a quick smile as she puts the postcards back in a pile. We talk for a few minutes more until the waiter brings our bills.

"I really have to pack," she says, retrieving money from her purse. We exchange addresses, the way travellers do.

"Lockhart. I've never heard of such a name."

"We're a rare breed."

Greta studies my face. She seems ready to say something, but doesn't. Her hand lingers after we shake, and she touches my shoulder lightly as she leaves.

I watch her walk along the beach in the growing darkness, toward the waterline. She is rather aimless, for someone with packing to do. She slips out of her sandals and lets the incoming waves sweep over her feet. The water must be cold, but she stands there still, as if frozen. An invitation. Or not.

I spot the paperback beside her coffee cup. Did she forget it on purpose? I pick it up, along with my knapsack, and start moving toward her.

"Your book."

"Oh. Thank you." She takes the book, but doesn't move.

"Is the water cold?" I say, to keep us talking.

"Not too bad. But the mosquitoes are really out now."

"Why don't you take my net? I'm on the pills. They can't hurt me."

"I couldn't do that."

"I insist. Really."

"All right. That's very kind." She touches my shoulder.

I'm pumped now. I'm playing with fire, but it feels good. We turn away toward the rooms, which all face the beach.

"I'm over here," I say, leading us along a pebble path and up the stairs. My mouth is dry. I wish the room had a mini-bar.

Once inside, Greta puts her sunhat and sweater on the desk, and sits on the bed. She runs her hands through the netting.

"Not too many holes," she says. Then, gathering it up, she tosses it over my head, like a superhero trying to snare an evil villain.

"Got you."

I laugh nervously, staring at her through the net's tiny squares. She moves closer, and starts to pull it off. One of the strands enters my mouth and catches on my ear. As she frees me, her warm fingers brush against my face. She runs her fingers through my mussed-up hair, patting it back in place. Then she brushes my face again. After all this, her kiss still catches me off-guard. It's warm, but dry. She pulls me toward her, and we sink onto the bed where we sit, silently kissing. She pushes me onto the bed and unbuttons my shirt.

"Do you have one?" she says.

"No."

"I do."

She uses my lips as a springboard to lift herself off the bed. She takes me by the hand, picking up her sweater and book. Perhaps it's the rush of evening breeze on my face, or the pressure of my feet on the paved walkway and the metal staircase, but by the time we reach Greta's room, I'm past the point of feeling alive. I just feel dread, a tightness in my chest. I need to stop this—now.

As Greta turns the key in the latch, she stares at the door for a moment. Then she turns to me.

"I'm sorry," she says, fighting tears. "I can't do this. I don't even know you. I'm very confused right now."

She kisses me on the cheek and slips into the room, snapping and bolting the door behind her. I stare at the closed door. This is what I wanted. So why do I feel so rejected? I walk back to my own room. The door is ajar. I had left it unlocked. I remember now. I push it open. The knapsack, with my camera, is gone. How could it happen so quickly? They must have been watching me. Maybe Greta was in on it. Maybe Frank set this up to teach me a lesson about locked doors and loose women. I look out from the balcony, and spot a flash of red. The guards are out of sight. Paid off, no doubt. I dash down the stairs and onto the beach. I can see a young girl far ahead, running with my knapsack at the water's edge. I start to run, even though I'll never catch her. Don't chase them, Frank said. But I do it anyway, just for a while, just until I can decide for myself when to stop.

Kiss it Better

"It's not working," Lisa said.

She let the receiver, which was part of a cat's back, fall heavily into the cat's body. I had told her to stick with Bell Canada, but Lisa wanted a designer telephone, something special for our first place together. She wanted a fresh start.

She rustled in my tool-box, coming up with a pair of side-cutters, which then slipped out of her hand and crashed on the floor. We were alone so she pouted, looking my way because I was the man, the one supposed to know about things. I didn't. In matters of home repair, we were equally incompetent. But, because I was the man, I refused to let on.

"Maybe the line isn't connected yet," I said. "Find the other phones and see if they work."

Lisa brightened, and pulled out her list.

I would have been happy for one-word labels on the boxes like "bedroom" and "kitchen." Lisa had insisted on a detailed list of contents. I waited now for her told-you-so smirk, but she was too excited to take the easy points.

"There's a phone in number 23," she said.

"There it is. Beside the stereo."

She hauled out the rotary phone, a gift from my parents who had a few extra ones lying around the cottage.

"Nothing," she said, plugging it in. "You were right, it's the line. Murray Lockhart: ace repairman."

I smiled.

Lisa went for details, cutting out lining-paper for the kitchen cupboards and putting away mismatched plates and glasses. I looked at the big picture—the relationship between the futon, the sofa, the stereo and the television. After placing the speakers on either side of the window, I picked up the sidecutters to trim the frayed wires and start fresh. I put the wires between the blades. Squeeze too much, and the blades would bite through the rubber into the hidden wires. Squeeze too lightly, and the rubber would simply stretch and tear when I tried to pull it off. I had to find the space between the rubber and the wires. Got it, first time.

"You are really good with tools," Lisa said, watching me from the galley-kitchen.

"I've got the magic touch," I said, blowing her a kiss.

"Hold that thought."

I did, but there were others too, like how many hours it had taken to master the art of sidecutting. I remembered how Dad would reach his arms around, taking my right hand into his. While my hands were soft and unblemished, his were dark and leathery, scarred from cuts that hadn't fully healed. His calluses rubbed roughly against my skin. He would show me how to hold the handle with three fingers on the outside and put my little finger on the inside. He would bend over to speak directly into my ear, his breath so full of grease, sweat and oil that I smelled the words more than heard them.

"Who's in charge, you or the tool?"

"Me." Because that was the right answer.

Dad would move his hands to my shoulders as I practised the trick. Open and close, open and close. My little finger worked the magic. I wanted so much to get it right, to make Dad proud. Once, after I had botched it again, I asked: "How do you know how much to squeeze?"

His hands tightened on my shoulders and then released.

"You just do. You'll get it. Don't worry."

Experience, he meant. Greasy hands, scarred palms, blotched fingers and chipped nails. After he disappeared into the garage, I kept at it. It was always one extreme or the other. Finally, I tossed the wire back on the workbench. I put a finger inside the sidecutters, squeezing gently. Open and close. I wondered how much pressure it would take to break the skin and draw blood, to scar, to get experience.

I shoved those old thoughts away and got back to unpacking. But the rotary phone rang a few minutes later, and the loud ringing seemed from another time, and made me think of my father again. I hadn't wanted the phone, but I didn't want to hurt my parents' feelings by refusing it.

"Oh hi," Lisa said. "You've just christened our phone line." Pause. "No, it's an old phone Murray got from his parents." Laughter. "I know. It's awful. It's right out of the sixties. I don't even remember how to dial."

It was Brie, Lisa's best friend, my arch rival. I could tell by the way Lisa's voice rose and fell so easily. On the phone with me, she spoke in measured and cautious tones. Judging from the tension rising in my chest, my rivalry with Brie hadn't ended when Lisa and I signed our lease. I still feared Brie would convince Lisa that she was really a lesbian. But it was even more than that: I resented Brie knew Lisa better, that they'd had a lifetime together already. I wanted to start out with Lisa free of history, mine as well as hers, and create something new.

"Brie's coming over in a while," Lisa said. "I invited her for dinner next week."

I could have insisted she ask before making plans that involved me. I could have put up a fuss or stomped around. But I didn't want Lisa to see Brie mattered that much to me. So all I said was, "Oh. All right."

With Brie on the way, Lisa went from box to box with her master list, unable to focus. I sensed her anxiety, her need for Brie's approval. By moving in with me, Lisa had shifted the balance of power among the three of us, and it wasn't clear yet how it would all shake down. It made me edgy too.

"Ow," she said, pulling her hand back from a box.

"Paper cut? Is it bleeding?"

"No. It just stings."

"Kiss it better?"

"Thanks, Dad. I'll be okay."

I knew she was just gearing up for Brie's arrival, putting on her "I am independent" armour. But Lisa had used the "kiss it better" line so often it had become our in-joke for requesting oral sex, either for her or for me. To have her ignore the reference—one of the few "traditions" we had established in our still-blossoming relationship—well, it stung.

"Whatever," I said, and turned away.

Brie showed up a half-hour later with new hair.

"Wild strawberry," she announced.

"Mmm-mmm-mmmm," said Lisa, patting the bristles on Brie's cropped head.

Peach, chocolate brown, orange, pink. Brie changed her hair colour almost as often as she fell in love. I wished she'd stick with one flavour and one girlfriend and give us some peace.

Brie stuck her housewarming gift on the refrigerator door: a "Dykes to Watch Out For" comic strip.

"It's not going to bother the boss, is it?"

"He's broken-in," said Lisa.

"Already? Too bad," said Brie. "I was hoping for a fight."

"With you? The human ice cream cone?" I said.

"You wanna lick?"

When she pushed her head up against me, her bristles fit under my chin. "Oh, Murray, you make me melt!" She leaned back, blowing me a kiss, swooning into Lisa's arms. Lisa, who was only a few inches shorter than I, captured her easily. They'd done this routine before and I gave them my best bored-look to prove it. Anything else would have egged them on.

"When you're finished, there's work to do."

"Relax," said Lisa. "We're halfway through the kitchen boxes." She picked up her master list from the kitchen-counter and waved it. "Only six more to go."

"Where's the vibrator?" Brie said, looking at the list in pseudo-innocence. "You know, the one I got for you? I could warm it up."

"I replaced it," I said, lying. "And the new one is re-charging. Thanks anyway."

The rotary phone rang once, my dad's signal to call back.

"What a sound," Brie said. "They were so offended they hung up."

"That was Murray's dad. They have this long-distance thing where he calls and hangs up and then Murray calls him back and hangs up, and then Burt calls him back again. Seriously. Burt doesn't want to get caught by the voicemail."

"Sounds like Pavlov's dog. Master rings. Murray jumps."

I did feel like a dog, but not because of my father's telephone ritual. It was how Lisa had set me up for ridicule that bothered me. I turned my back on both of them, and my father, and opened a new box.

Brie moved into the living-room, and rooted through a stack of prints leaning against the wall. She found *The Broadsword and the Beast*, a promotional poster for a Jethro Tull album. I hadn't had it up in years, but it was a reminder of my past that I couldn't quite part with.

"Jethro Tull, Murray? Lisa and I listened to that guy when we were twelve. Look at this sword. It's so phallic." She leaned the poster with its face against the wall and then backed away slowly, as if the beast were about to leap off the page.

"Please don't tell anyone I even saw this."

"Don't worry," Lisa said. "Jethro's going in the trash this week."

I didn't want the poster up anyway, but they didn't leave much room for an honourable exit.

"Tull is a them, not a him," I said.

Brie moved over to box fifteen, pulling out a framed photo of Lisa and me.

"All you need is a mantel." She looked around the room, finger to her lips in mock reflection. "Let's see."

"Hand it over," I said.

She put her hands behind her back.

"Left or right?"

"Left," said Lisa from the kitchen. "She always chooses left."

"Not fair! Start over."

I reached both arms around her waist to grab the frame. We struggled a moment, and my hands brushed up against her ass.

"Oh, Murray," she said, breathlessly, pushing up against my crotch. "I can feel your broadsword pressing against me."

It wasn't true, but as she pressed, I did start to get hard. She felt it too. I could see it in her face, how her eyes narrowed and her lips curled into a smirk.

"I guess that makes you the beast," I said. Just as I started to pry her fingers off the frame, she opened her hand, and the frame dropped to the floor. The glass cracked, and a large shard fell off so the photograph was half-exposed.

"Thanks a lot," I said, bending down to pick it up.

"I'll clean it up," she said, pushing my hand out of the way. She reached out too quickly and cut her finger.

"Fuck," she said, sucking it. "Leese. You know how I hate blood. Get me a band-aid, will you?"

"I'll get some ice," Lisa said. "Murray, can you get the band-aids?" She threw me the master list. "All the bathroom boxes are down the hall."

I found them easily, and returned to find Brie with her feet up on box 51. Lisa sat beside her, pressing an ice cube wrapped in a dish towel against the cut.

"Shall I call 911 or take you straight to the morgue?" I said.

Brie patted her finger in the dish towel, and then held it out for the band-aid.

"Kiss it better first," she said, pointing it toward Lisa.

This was a defining moment for me, and Lisa knew it. Behind Brie's childish gesture was defiance—a demand for intimacy that would place her above me. Apart from that, of course, I wondered now where Lisa had come up with the phrase, if it had some sexual connotation with Brie. It was more history I wanted to erase.

"I don't want your cooties," Lisa said, dabbing the blood

with the cloth before putting on the band-aid. She struck just the right tone for Brie to save face. I chose not to gloat, which to my mind was an even more powerful response.

"All right, I'm history," said Brie, waving her bandaged finger. "I don't want to keep Fido from calling Daddy back."

"I'll look forward to seeing you for dinner next week," I said. The unexpected magnanimity had the desired effect: her mouth opened slightly. But she turned the tables again, surprising me with a genuine smile. She blew Lisa a kiss, and then when the door closed behind her, Lisa and I sat down in the living-room, suddenly becalmed. Both of us felt it, this silence descending.

"Let's get rid of that phone before it rings again," I said, only half-joking. After I unplugged it, Lisa installed the cat phone and ordered pizza. We cleaned up the broken glass. After dinner, we left the dishes until morning, and crawled into bed.

"Kiss it better?" I whispered.

She stroked my face with the back of her hand.

"It's like sandpaper. You're not going anywhere near me with that stubble."

What I heard was: *I don't trust you to give me an orgasm with your tongue.* Or perhaps, *it would be so much easier if you were a woman. You would know what to do. Your cheeks would be soft and unthreatening.*

She guided my hand between her legs. Is this how it was with Brie all those years ago? I couldn't bear to ask.

I moved my finger in little circles, trying to listen to her body's responses, trying to keep my heart open.

"Can you stop for a while? I've lost you."

At the sound of her voice, my finger stopped, and I stayed perfectly still.

"Let me show you."

She placed a finger on top of mine, showing me how much pressure to use, which paths to take. She playfully locked my finger inside her body and then released it. Open and close.

For a second I was back at the cottage, my finger in the side-cutters.

"You don't have to go so fast. Sometimes less is more."

We found a rhythm together. Soon her breath came in little spurts and her body started to shake and tremble. I wished she would trust enough to let me touch her on my own, but she didn't. When she reached a climax, it was her victory, not mine. Afterwards, we both saw the drops of blood on my finger. She was embarrassed, and then moved to tears as I sucked them off. She looked at me with such affection, but all I could think was how I wanted that blood to be mine.

Civilization

When I got home from work at Friends of Africa, I wanted to disappear into the den, warm up the computer and resume my game of Civilization. After two weeks and 463 turns, Shaka—my Zulu warrior—had experienced several major setbacks in his bid for world domination. With their short-handled spears, Shaka's warriors were experts in close combat in the early going, but by the late seventeenth century, Joan d'Arc's musketeers outclassed them. Now, in the mid twentieth century, the American F-15s would be in the picture soon, and I wanted desperately for Shaka to prepare for the new threat.

But in a few minutes Lisa would arrive home exhausted from another day spent counselling abused women at the shelter. An hour later, she would leave again for a march to commemorate the women killed in Montreal in 1989. It would not do to be found playing Civ, a game she referred to as Rape and Pillage. Not when our relations had been so icy this week. My eyes strayed to the white ribbon held on to the refrigerator door by the "Practise Random Acts of Kindness" magnet. She'd wanted me to wear the ribbon—the symbol of men determined to make the world safer for women. I refused because I thought men should also be allowed to march.

"If men are the problem, they have to be part of the solution."

"Women need to march alone. This is your way to help," she'd said, holding up the ribbon. Then she'd stuck it to the fridge door. Her choice of magnet, I'm certain, was no accident. It stayed there all week, an unresolved conflict just below the surface. The combination of her exhaustion from work and my apparent intransigence around the white ribbon had led to several weeks without sex. Even touching, which had been so integral to our connection, was becoming off-limits.

So instead of indulging in the virtual warfare of Civ, I launched a campaign to win back Lisa's affections. Since I knew she would be tired and rushed, I started making Kraft Dinner—her favourite comfort food. Then I pulled King Crimson out of the CD player just after "Sex, Sleep, Eat, Dream" finished and put on Sarah McLachlan's *Solace* album. These strategic acts of kindness, I was certain, would go a long way toward melting Lisa's heart. I thought about putting on the ribbon, but it felt too manipulative—even for me.

I had just put the macaroni in the boiling water when the telephone rang once: my dad's signal. I hesitated to ring back because I suspected another letter was in the offing. With the sudden emergence of a witness to his traffic accident last fall, we had written a new series of letters to his broker, the insurance company, the police—anyone he thought might listen. He provided the raw words, and I shaped them, using my experience as a direct-mail writer to strike the right notes and tone down his "I fought for this country to preserve truth and justice" lines.

When he last called, he was contemplating a letter to the other insurance company. "I've been through hell," he'd said. "I've had health problems and everything else, and this guy's got off scot-free. We know he's guilty now, and they should do something about it." I just didn't know if I had the energy to lead the charge in my father's battle anymore. Of course, I would never tell Lisa this. After only a month in therapy, she had been quick to diagnose my relationship with my father as co-dependent. "His problems are self-generated," she'd said. "He's got that rash on his chest because he won't let the accident go. And you're *enabling* him by writing those letters."

Yet it was precisely because I felt judged by Lisa that I felt honour-bound to continue the letters, as much as I resented them. So I rang back once, hung up and waited—pen and paper in hand—for the return call on his dime. When it came, Dad spoke like he always did, as if the conversation were already in progress.

"I just saw something for Pearl Harbour. Virgie, when was it on?" His voice trailed off into the living-room. In the distance, I could hear my mother say, "Tomorrow at nine."

"Tomorrow night at nine," Dad said.

"It's the anniversary tomorrow."

"Yes, that's right. December 7th. Hard to believe. That's why Ted and I joined up, you know. After Pearl Harbour, we both wanted to be in the navy. He never made it back, though. He was in the galley starting dinner when the torpedo hit."

Silence.

"You might not have been born, you know, if I hadn't made it back. Or you would have been somebody else."

"You said the movie's on at nine? I'll write that down."

"I can tape it in case you miss it. Then you can watch it when you come out here."

"Okay."

"You got your tickets yet?"

"Yesterday. We'll be there on the twenty-second and stay until the day after New Year's."

"That's not much time," said my mother, who picked up the other extension.

"I only get three weeks of holidays."

"All right then," Dad said. "Better get off now. We'll see you soon enough."

He hung up, but Mom was still on the line.

"How's Lisa?"

"Fine. What are you up to?"

"We've having a surprise birthday party tomorrow. I'm baking the cake."

"That sounds like fun."

"Well, I'd better let you go."

I hung up, thinking every day was an anniversary for something, feeling sad that so little of consequence exchanged among the three of us, and relieved there was no new letter to invent tonight.

A few minutes later, I heard Lisa's key in the lock. At first, I thought her face was wet with melted snow, but from the puffy look in her eyes, I realized she had been crying. Once she removed her winter coat, I reached out to her, but she pushed me away.

"I'm sorry. I don't want to be touched. It's just more stimulation."

She looked without comment at the dinner underway, and then zapped a mug full of water in the microwave. She dropped a bag of herbal tea into the steaming mug, and curled up on the futon in the living-room. I should have had the mug ready.

I dropped a tablespoon of butter into the water to keep it from boiling over, and sat down at a respectful distance across the room until she was ready to talk.

"There was a new woman in the shelter today. She came in last night. She's from some African country. She lost both her children in a war. The army stole her son. They made him cut off people's hands. Her daughter...."

Lisa stopped, bowing her head into the mug held tightly in her hands.

After two months of living together, I knew Lisa just wanted me to sit silently, "holding space" as she processed the day. In theory, my job was simply to stay present, and not offer advice or comfort. In practice, my mind often wandered back to the game. If I could just build another barracks, I could upgrade my obsolete warriors and crush my opponents.

"Forget it. I can tell you're not listening. You're in your head again."

She got up and shut the music off just as the song "Shelter" was starting. I got up too because the water was boiling over again, but she beat me to the stove. She turned the heat off, and got a strainer out of the cupboard to drain the macaroni. I couldn't keep up with the emotions coming at me from all directions: anger, resentment, shame, frustration. With my strategy in complete disarray, I saw no reason not to return to Civ in the den.

"Excuse me. I'm going to rape and pillage for a while."

"I hope you get your balls cut off."

I entered the den, shut the door firmly behind me, and powered up the game. I had once tried to interest Lisa in Civ by playing the role of Gandhi, and shooting for a cultural, rather than a military, victory. Even then, she disapproved. She shook her head as I explained how I was racking up cultural points by creating wonders-of-the-world.

"It doesn't matter whether you're Gandhi or someone else, you're still trying to take over the world."

I didn't see anything wrong with that. Having won Lisa from the clutches of her lesbian friend Brie, I needed new worlds to conquer. And with Lisa off sex these days, and increasingly standoffish even around touching, the game allowed me to keep focused rather than let my eyes wander too much. It was an investment in our relationship.

Ten minutes after I got new granaries for my cities, Lisa knocked tentatively on the door and stepped inside, waving a white dish-towel over her head.

"Truce?"

At the touch of her arm on my shoulder, I saved my game of Rape and Pillage and turned my thoughts back to a possible sexual encounter later that evening. As we settled down to our Kraft Dinner, Lisa made eye contact.

"So how was your day saving the world?" she said.

I'd spent the morning fighting with the printer about his quote for business-size envelopes for our current fundraising package. In the afternoon, I updated my action plan, went to a staff meeting and caught up with my filing. The world saved, I'd gone home.

"We got the go-ahead for a new fundraising campaign on female genital mutilation. They also agreed to send me to a conference on FGM in Montreal in February so I can get a feel for the issue."

"They're sending a man?"

"It's my job. I'm writing the package and co-ordinating the launch of the campaign next fall."

"It's not a spaceship. It's a human rights issue."

The phone rang, and Lisa—knowing my father's ritual—waited for the second ring before answering. To her surprise, it was my dad. He must have reasoned I would still be home.

"I've got some ideas for that letter."

I scribbled them all down, listening without comment and then hung up a few minutes later.

"What was that all about?"

"The usual."

"More letters, you mean. Why do you keep this up?"

"If he wrote them himself, they'd think he was a nutcase."

Lisa's raised eyebrow said, "my point exactly."

"If he spent ten minutes in the shelter, he'd find out what's important."

"He was in a war. You don't need to teach him anything about priorities."

"What about your priorities? Every time the phone rings, you jump. You should see yourself the way I do. Have some self-respect."

I couldn't speak. When I'm soft and loving, my eyes can melt bra straps. But in those moments where conflicting emotions are fused together, where the anger and hurt run so deep that I can't reach or understand them, all I can do is glare. I knew the glare had poisoned my relationships with Cassandra, Nicky and Paulette so I was determined to express myself more verbally with Lisa. That's why, when the glare came over me, pummelling Lisa against her chair, my anger toward her faded instantly, replaced by remorse. But the damage had been done. Lisa touched her lips, as if to check for blood. She got up slowly, walked into the bedroom and shut the door.

She would have to emerge soon, and I wondered how I

could possibly make it up to her with words. I wanted to invent another look, one that would heal her wounds—the ones I had just inflicted, and all the others inflicted on her and all women by all men throughout time. I took the white ribbon off the fridge door, then, and trembling, pinned it to my shirt. I stood in the hall, waiting, hoping my face looked as contrite as I felt inside.

When Lisa came out, and saw me wearing the ribbon, her eyes narrowed in disbelief.

"If you'd been wearing that when I got home, it would have meant something. Now...."

You've got it all wrong, I wanted to say. *I couldn't wear it before. Now I really mean it.*

She pulled on her winter clothes, grabbed her keys and left. I walked back to the sunroom, waiting for her to appear below. Standing in the darkness, I wondered about holding a "take back the night" march on such a miserable evening. Anyone with any sense was indoors. Even the homeless were tucked away in sheltered alleys. There would be no-one out there to see these women, no men to take back the night from.

The little truck hadn't been around to salt the sidewalks yet so Lisa walked tentatively down the street. I watched until she slipped and slid into darkness. In a few minutes, she would meet other women at the Jack Purcell Community Centre, and they would march up Elgin Street to the Human Rights Memorial, chanting slogans. They would come back down Elgin to Minto Park, where the city put up that stone to commemorate the Montreal Massacre. They would stand in the freezing rain, trying to keep their candles lit. Someone, maybe a local politician eager to score points, would speak out on violence against women. Someone else would read a poem. They would stand in silence for a few moments. Then they would all go home.

I would have hot chocolate waiting for Lisa upon her return. That would be something. In the meantime, I had my father's letter to write. I sat at the computer, but instead returned to my game of Civ. After Joan d'Arc's torpedo penetrated my ship's hull, I closed my eyes. I could almost see the men below the water-line tumbling from their bunks as salt water gushed through the gaping hole. Friends and comrades perished. Some were swept out to sea. Others were thrown against the bulkhead, breaking arms and legs. As the engines shut down and temperatures began to rise, the survivors waded in darkness through the rising water and oil, sweating from the heat, coughing on thick smoke, one hand on the back of the man in front as they sought to reach the hatch. Yes, they would survive, but nothing would ever be the same.

Circumcision through Words

As I unlace my skates after the game, listening to the guys talk about basement renovations, the new baby or French-language training, it's like I've stumbled onto a gathering of male elders speaking an ancient tongue. It doesn't help that I'm an un-circumcised Gentile playing in the local Jewish Men's Hockey League. I can sense their curious glances in the shower. No-one says anything because this is my first year in the league. They don't know me well enough to tease or torment.

Jeff nods, slinging his bag over his shoulder on the way out. He's married to a woman at my office, which is how I heard about the league. We go through the perfunctory nod-of-the-head after every game.

Jeff was the one who checked the roster and got me a ride with Darren, the star of our team. The other players admire his skill, his physique, his bravado. But mostly I think, they envy his freedom. He's a mechanic for Canadian Tire, and picks up young women who arrive alone at the shop. As Darren entertains the fellows with his latest sexual exploits, they drink cold water from their bottles to quench their burning hearts. Like me, Darren doesn't quite fit in, but he's accepted because the others recognize him as the man they once were, or wanted to be.

"I talked to my cousin Larry last week," Darren says. "He says he's trying to regrow his foreskin. He walks around all day with weights on his dick. I shit you not. He's into some men's group that's trying to"—he puts on an effeminate voice—'reclaim his manhood that was lost during circumcision.'"

The other guys shudder, but I listen up. I'm going to Montreal tomorrow for a conference on female genital mutilation so the topic seems strangely appropriate.

"I've heard of that," someone says. "They do it because

they think it makes sex better."

"Knowing Larry and his wife, I don't think that's an issue. If you're not gettin' it, it doesn't matter how much skin you've got."

He gets a laugh.

"Don't you try it, Saul," Darren says, calling out to the young guy across the room. Saul looks barely nineteen and I have no idea how he ended up in a men's league. Apart from his youth, he's religious, overweight and slurs his speech. All that makes him the perfect target for Darren.

"No way."

"What, are you calling my cousin stupid?"

"No. I didn't say that."

"Because he's a big guy, Saul. He'll whip your ass for saying that."

Some guys laugh, while others shake their heads in embarrassment for Saul.

"So have you got laid yet, Saul? Someone came into the shop today. An African princess. I could get her number for you."

"Okay."

"She likes her men big, though, with lots of skin. You think you've got enough skin, Saul? Or should I get Larry to lend you his weights?"

"Oh come on."

More laughter. As I zip up my hockey bag, an argument with Lisa earlier that evening runs through my head:

"Why don't you stand up for Saul?"

"You don't do that. It's not part of the culture."

"Jewish culture?"

"Locker-room culture."

"So no-one cuts this Darren down to size? He just gets away with it?"

"I suppose so."

"That's what's wrong with the world, Murray. There are too many Darrens out there, and no-one is willing to take them on."

79

I didn't respond. I knew she was on edge about her sister. Margo hadn't returned Lisa's calls or emails in a week. Worrying about Saul was a way to avoid worrying about Margo.

I look at Saul packing equipment into his bag with his head down. It would be out of place for me to defend Saul. One of the Jewish guys should take the lead or Saul should defend himself. Another part of me thinks I should say something. Anything. And then the decision is made: Darren is packed and ready to go, giving Saul a reprieve until next week.

Darren fills the twenty-minute drive home from the arena with more talk of his sexual adventures. When he drops me off, he yells out his window: "See you next week, Billy!"

"My name is Murray," I say, but the window is already up.

I crash and bang my way up to our second-floor apartment with my hockey bag and sticks, expecting to find Lisa sound asleep. Instead, she's up in bed, writing furiously in her journal.

"My mother called the restaurant and they said Margo quit her job last week. I'm really worried she's been drinking again. Will you go by her place after the conference, just to check up on her?"

Her voice had broken a little, and once again I was surprised at the emotion. In the same room together, Lisa and her sister can't show each other any love. Apart, though, Lisa frets about her all the time. Sometimes, when Lisa talks in her sleep, I pick up the thread of her nightmares. She sees Margo driving home drunk and slamming into a hydro pole, killing herself just the way their father did. Most of the time, though, her mouth voices words I can't make out. I don't wake her because I think she needs to work it through, but I do put my arm around her until her breathing slips back to normal. This has become the best part of our relationship— the silent comforting. We only have conflict when we're awake.

80

"She's probably just unplugged the phone or gone on holiday."

"Are you saying you won't go by her place?"

"I didn't say that. I'm just saying there's nothing to worry about."

"That's what you keep saying about your father too, and he's about to keel over at any moment."

I turn away, too tired to engage her.

"I'm sorry. I'm just worried."

The tears come freely now, and she lets me hold her. In these moments, when she reaches out, I want to cradle her in my arms like a child. I want to heal those hurts.

"I'm sure she's okay."

"Stop saying that," she says, pushing me away. I get up, frustrated and angry.

"Don't you want her to be okay?"

"What a fucking stupid thing to say."

I walk out of the bedroom and sleep on the futon, knowing my distance is more terrible for her than words. In the morning, I get up early and dress quietly. Before I leave for the bus, I scribble a peace offering: a promise to call on Margo. This makes me feel better, but I still hate to leave with unresolved, twisted feelings.

I doze on the bus, waking only when it pulls into the station. A quick ride on the Metro and I reach the university, finding the conference-room without any trouble. I register, picking up a binder and a "Hello, my name is..." sticker. At a quiet seat in the back, I take off my winter coat. I print my name, stick the tag to the lapel, and then watch others file in. They are mostly black women. They arrive in groups of twos and threes. If Darren were here, he'd be planning a *ménage à trois*. I presume they're all Africans, or African-Canadians. Have they bonded so quickly or did they already know each other? A few black men arrive, followed by a handful of white women. As the only white man in the room, I suddenly feel conspicuous so I open my binder and review the agenda.

After the morning plenary and lunch, I've signed up for the Health Effects workshop.

The chairperson, a matronly African with grizzled hair, taps the microphone. In both official languages, she urges people to find a place so we can begin. A few seats down from me, a young black woman with cornrow braids sits by herself. She slips her knapsack onto the empty chair beside her, as if she's saving it for someone, but no-one joins her.

In the plenary, the chair introduces Doctor Ogunsola, an African physician originally from Nigeria who now practises in Toronto. He's heavy-set, and talks with a good deal of swagger. Many women whisper in their seats, shaking their heads at this display. Even the chairperson looks uncomfortable sitting at the same table with him.

"Women have to start taking responsibility for this horrific practice," says Doctor Ogunsola. "The African men won't talk about it, as you know too well. It is up to you. Mothers are to blame. They must be educated."

"Who are you to blame the mothers?" a woman in the audience shouts back at him. A few other women cry out in agreement.

"Who would you blame then? The fathers?" the doctor retorts. His eyes search the crowd to find the heckler.

"The doctors," someone else shouts.

"I don't think we need to blame anyone," the chairperson says. "Please let the doctor finish his remarks. There will be plenty of time for discussion in the workshops."

"Thank you, Madame Chair," the doctor says. He gloats a little, pulling the microphone closer to his mouth.

"In my practice, I have seen too many young girls living in Canada who have been forced to undergo this barbaric procedure. There is no excuse for it in this country. None whatsoever."

"What do you know about it?" a voice calls out. It's the young woman with the braids. She stands up. "Let me tell you something. All of my African friends in Toronto had it done. My mother thought she was protecting me, but she made me an outcast. My friends rejected me. If I had the choice, I would have it done today."

As she sits down, the room is filled with an angry buzz, but this time it's not directed at the doctor. "You are a stupid girl," someone calls out. Heads turn toward the young woman who sits there defiantly, returning all the hard gazes. The African doctor shakes his head at the woman, in a sad, patronizing way. "You do not understand what you're saying," he says into the microphone.

"Please. Everyone," says the chairperson. "This is a very sensitive issue. We know that. That's why we're here. To work together to find solutions."

After a few minutes, the plenary continues. One panelist, a white woman from a UN agency, talks about FGM as a human rights issue. Another panelist, an African woman from Kenya, talks about an alternative to FGM called "circumcision through words." It's an approach that Friends of Africa has already started to support in Tanzania—a week-long rite of passage for young women that finishes with a "coming-of-age day" where the entire community joins in for music, dance and feasting.

It's all interesting, but by this time, most people can't sit still. A few steal glances at the woman with the cornrow braids, sneering or shaking their heads with pity. When the woman looks my way, I see the name on her tag is Kiddisti. I try to be affirming with a small, tight-lipped smile. She smiles back.

Kiddisti and I sit together with our buffet lunch in a far corner of the cafeteria, away from the others who clump together in the centre of the room. Her body, which I had thought was simply slender, is flat and angular, almost anorexic. Her long face and her mouth, with its crooked bottom teeth and thin lips, make her appear tough, but I can see sadness in her dark eyes. Sadness and vulnerability. My heart flutters a little, sitting alone with her. If someone came to join us, I would tell them to go somewhere else. Only outsiders belong here.

"These women, they make me sick," Kiddisti says. "No-one ever says anything out loud, but it's like they have a club. If you're not mutilated, you can't join. You don't even have the right to talk to them. This is what makes me so angry. I have felt this way all my life, always pushed to the outside."

She stabs a piece of cauliflower.

"I have never felt at home in Canada. So I finally went back to Eritrea two years ago, to see if I could live there. I hadn't been home since I left in the nineteen-seventies."

"You left when the war started with Ethiopia?"

"That's right." Her eyes search for signs of judgment. "I had an uncle in Toronto, and he took us in—my mother, brother and me. But I still had lots of family in Asmara. I went to see them. They were polite, but it was obvious I didn't fit in. My accent, my clothes. Behind their smiles, they were angry. My aunts had all lost sons in the war. They never forgave my mother for leaving. They resented me for being alive. It was clear to me I could never go back."

"That's very sad."

"I'm over it now. I'm happy here at McGill doing African Studies."

I'm not convinced, but I don't challenge her.

"So why did they send you to this conference?" she says.

"To learn more about FGM. It's the theme for our fundraising campaign next fall."

"The theme," she repeats.

"I'll be getting one of our partners to help. She runs an organization called Whole Women. I met her when I went to Tanzania."

Silence for a moment, as we finish up our lunch.

"Do you have any Africans working with you?" she says.

"We used to. She went back to Nigeria."

"Huh," she says, with a sneer. "Good for her."

There's another awkward silence so I reach into my pocket for a business card.

"If you ever come to Ottawa, stop by the office."

Our fingers touch as we exchange the card, and it sends a shiver of possibility down my spine.

"Thanks. I will."

"We should go now. It's getting on. Which workshop are you in?"

"Education Strategies."

"Me too," I say, lying.

She smiles warmly.

"Good. It will be nice to have a friend in the room."

As we enter the workshop, my heart sinks a little. Doctor Ogunsola is there. Kiddisti chooses a chair directly opposite the doctor, and scrapes it loudly across the floor. He looks up from his binder then lowers his gaze again. The other six or seven participants, all African women, look curiously as I sit beside Kiddisti. The fiercest glance is from the young woman two seats down from Kiddisti. With her light skin, I wonder if she's Ethiopian, and if this will create another conflict with Kiddisti. I'm glad there's an empty chair between them.

A middle-aged African woman standing at the front writes "Education Strategies" in block letters on a flipchart, then turns to face everyone at the table.

"Welcome everyone. My name is Dorothy, and I'm the facilitator. Can we have a go-around to introduce ourselves? Just your name and your organization. I'd also like a volunteer to take notes as we go along." She sits down and picks up a pen. As the names are called out, she ticks them off a list. The light-skinned woman, whose name is Gelila, offers to take notes.

Dorothy scans her list after I say my name aloud.

"Murray Lockhart. I don't seem to have you here. Is this where you're supposed to be?"

I can feel everyone focused on me. Even Kiddisti has turned her head slightly, waiting for my answer.

"This is where I want to be."

"Fine then."

After the go-around, Dorothy recaps the presentation from the Kenyan woman on "circumcision through words." She asks us to consider how to transfer the spirit of this approach to those African communities in Canada that still believe in FGM.

"I think we need to go straight to the girls themselves," says Gelila. "We need to empower them to make their own decisions, to show them they have choices."

Doctor Ogunsola shakes his head.

"No, no, no. It's very well to say that, but the fact of the matter is, these girls are like sheep. They will do what their mothers and their grandmothers tell them. You have to reach the mothers first. In my practice...."

"We know all about your practice," says Kiddisti. "You obviously treat women like animals."

"Please," Dorothy says. "Can we stay on the topic?"

"Your mother was right to protect you," Doctor Ogunsola says, looking squarely at Kiddisti. "But I don't know if you deserved it."

Kiddisti's eyes well up with tears. Several of the women draw in their breath sharply, and Gelila slams her pen down on the table.

"Who are you to say that to her?" I say, my voice shaking. "You call yourself a doctor?"

Now Ogunsola's eyes well up with tears.

"I am sorry," he says to Kiddisti. "I feel very strongly about this. My wife took our daughter to her village in Nigeria. My mother-in-law went behind our backs. They used a razor blade, and Ajayi died. She bled to death." His voice chokes at the words, and he lowers his face toward the table.

A hushed, uncomfortable silence fills the room.

"I am sorry for you," Kiddisti says, finally, holding back tears. Dr. Ogunsola nods without looking up.

"Why don't we take a break for a few minutes?" Dorothy

says. Before I can get up, Gelila has offered Kiddisti a tissue to dry her eyes.

"It's horrible, isn't it?" Gelila says. "How this affects everyone in different ways."

Kiddisti nods, dabbing her eyes.

"I'm going to the washroom," Gelila says. "Do you want to come?"

Kiddisti follows her out of the room. The other women file out as well, leaving Doctor Ogunsola and me alone in the room. The doctor keeps his head down, dabbing his eyes with a handkerchief.

"I'm sorry," I say, quietly.

He doesn't respond. Say something, I think. Anything. But he doesn't look up. He leaves the room with his head bowed. The empty room reinforces the hollow feeling inside my gut so I walk aimlessly in the hall for a few minutes. Then I remember Margo. She's not there so I leave a message on her answering machine that says I'll try again later, before I head home. Once I return to the meeting-room, Gelila has filled the empty chair next to Kiddisti, and the two of them are talking quietly together. They seem to have become fast friends. The other women arrive, but the doctor's chair remains empty.

"Doctor Ogunsola decided to leave," Dorothy says. "He said it was too much for him. He didn't feel it was right for him to stay."

Several of the women cluck in protest, while others nod their heads sadly. A few glance at me, as if to say, "Why did you push him over the edge? Who do you think you are?" Kiddisti and Gelila start talking even more intensely. I wish now that I had left too. For the next hour, the women talk about ways to reach elders, mothers and children. They talk about reaching African doctors, community-development workers and politicians. I offer a few words of advice about influencing news media, but for the most part, I just listen. By the end, Gelila has filled five sheets of flipchart paper with ideas and strategies. As the workshop draws to a close, Dorothy asks for a volunteer to present our report to plenary.

"I nominate Kiddisti," Gelila says. A few of the other women nod in approval.

"Oh, I don't know."

"I can help you make sense of my writing."

"Yes, you do it," one of the women says.

"All right," Kiddisti says, smiling shyly.

"That's settled then," Dorothy says. "Good work everyone. See you in plenary in fifteen minutes." With those words, the women start talking among themselves again. Kiddisti and Gelila remove the flipchart paper that's taped to the walls. I fold up my binder, gather my coat and leave the room quickly, unnoticed.

At the pay telephone in the hall, I try Margo again. This time she's home.

"I was hoping you'd call back soon." Her voice is tense. "I've been on the phone for the past half-hour listening to all of Lisa's messages."

"She's been worried."

"She shouldn't have been. You can tell her I've been away with Darren in Florida."

"Darren?"

"You sound surprised. He's an old boyfriend. Lisa knows him."

"He's not a mechanic, is he?"

Margo laughs. "A photographer."

"What about your job?"

"I got a better one, closer to home. I start tomorrow."

"I told her it was something like that."

"She should have listened to you. You're the voice of reason."

After I hang up, I see other participants head back into the main room for the final plenary. Gelila and Kiddisti are walking together like old friends. I decide to cut out early and head home. As I button up my coat, I see the name tag still stuck on the lapel of my suit. The upside-down letters look strange, and I silently mouth my name the way it should sound, as if to reassure myself the two words are not part of some foreign language beyond my grasp.

Spirit Speak

After only 30 hours of playing Omni On-line, I was wandering as an invisible spirit in the virtual world of Britannia, looking for a healer or a shrine to bring me back to life. I was Magrippe, a Warlock. I had bought a spell-scroll and garlic from a magic shop a few turns back to create protective armour. Before I could recite the spell, I was felled by a swordsman. If I tried to communicate, the other players in the game—except those who knew Spirit Speak—would hear my words as incomprehensible wails. I wasn't worried. No-one stayed dead too long.

The telephone rang once, jarring me out of Britannia and back into the den of our Ottawa apartment. It was my father's signal, but I chose not to call him back. The phone rang again, this time long enough for the voicemail to click on. It must have been something urgent for my father to pay for a long-distance call, or it was someone else. I sat at the computer, torn between continuing my search for rebirth and checking the message. I kept playing. Lisa would be home from work soon and I wanted to take advantage of her absence. The time I spent on computer games was the last major source of contention between us, and I was determined not to break the spell of domestic bliss that enveloped us.

Since Lisa had decided not to renew her contract at the women's shelter, much of the stress in our lives had melted away. She smiled more. She accepted hugs and massages. Brie, her best friend and my chief rival for her affections, had fallen in love again, and was not over at our place so often. Even better, Lisa had decided against travelling with Brie and Teresa to Indonesia this summer, which I took as renewed faith in our relationship. Talk therapy was helping her make sense of her life. I was a paternal figure—a fill-in for her dead father—and the knowledge seemed to soothe her, because we were making love again. She had discovered "energy work" too, and was now planning to get trained in polarity therapy. A small part of me felt left behind by all her progress, but I didn't dwell on it. Work was busy. Summer was coming. And I had my life in Britannia.

When I heard Lisa at the front door, I left Britannia and switched over to my email inbox. She came into the den a few minutes later. She kissed me, then collapsed in the spare chair next to the computer.

"There's a message from your dad. He recited a poem about Ted. He wants you to type it up so he can enter it into a poetry contest. When he's thanking you for your help, he says, 'You're the best friend a fellow could have, Ted.'"

"It was just a slip of the tongue. Or maybe it was part of the poem."

"No. You listen to it. It's eerie. It's like he's talking to a ghost. Ted died 60 years ago. It's so sad your dad can't let him go. Apart from all that, it's one god-awful poem. I hope you can change his mind about submitting it. He's really going to be embarrassed."

"It's what he wants to do. It's not going to hurt anyone."

"It's probably a scam. They'll give him an award just to get him to buy the book. You know how these things work."

"I thought you didn't like it when I tried to parent my dad. You're always telling me I'm protecting him."

"You're protecting him right now. You're not willing to tell him the truth about his poem."

"It can't be that bad."

"It's bad, Murray. Maybe you can at least suggest some changes to make it less sentimental."

"It's his poem, not mine. Besides, he won't believe me. He only hears what he wants to hear."

"All right. I can see I'm not getting anywhere with you." She turned to leave. "I've got to eat before therapy. What are you doing tonight?"

"I got the draft of the direct-mail letter from the woman in Tanzania. It needs some work."

She stopped in the doorway. "It's not okay to touch your dad's poem, but you're going to edit this woman's letter."

"It's not the same thing."

"It's worse. You asked this woman to write the letter, and now you're going to change her words. I'd like to see what she came up with." She paused. "It can't be that bad."

She walked back and sat in the chair again.

I read parts of it, expecting Lisa to laugh at the bureaucratic tone. She didn't. "It's not that bad. She's really getting to the core of the issue."

"I am going to have to touch it up."

"But not too much, right?"

"No, not too much. Just a little off the top."

She kissed me then, and left to fix her sandwich.

I sat there, baffled. Surely Lisa could see how awful the letter was? Couldn't she?

I had been forced to invite Rhobi Juba to write the first draft as part of a new "inclusive practices" policy at Friends of Africa. It was no longer enough to get our partners to approve fundraising letters that went out in their name, they actually had to help write them. This was all in the name of "building capacity in our African partners."

I had asked Rhobi to contrast her own family's experience of female genital mutilation with the painless coming-of-age ritual for young girls known as "circumcision through words." Instead, she focused on the rehabilitation of mutilators. Mistake. I did not think our target audience—urban professional women with children—would want to help former mutilators become hairdressers. I had already started a complete re-write of the letter, risking the wrath of Rhobi, my politically correct colleagues and now Lisa too.

I clicked out of the email program and Rhobi's words vanished from sight. I retrieved the new draft, typed in Dark Courier—a font that suggested Rhobi might have actually banged out the letter herself on a beat-up typewriter in Tanzania. Dark Courier also sounded mystical, which appealed to me. I was Magrippe, casting a spell on affluent Canadian women to read this letter and send us money.

```
Dear Friend,

One day, when I was six years old, my
mother called me inside our small house in
Talime, a village in Tanzania. "Rhobi,"
she said, smiling. "Today is the day you
become a woman." Led by my mother and
grandmother, I was taken to the home of
the midwife. I wasn't nervous. My mother
told me it wouldn't hurt. But it did hurt.
Thirty years later, it still hurts.

I am not alone. Every day, in many African
countries, six thousand girls are
"circumcised" in the name of tradition.
This practice is more properly known as
female genital mutilation, or FGM.

I do not blame my mother for what she did.
But I've dedicated my life to educating
women so they no longer hurt their
daughters in the name of tradition. Won't
you help me?

Please turn over...
```

I kept going, adding more details, building momentum to the pitch for support. But in the end, I was dissatisfied. I needed something more to bring it to life. I stared at the screen for a few minutes, then gave up for the night. Lisa would be home soon and I wanted to get my father's poem out of the way and resume my search for a healer in Britannia.

It was a sentimental poem, but I still teared up as Dad

93

choked over his words, at how he got confused at the end about my name. I so wished to make his pain disappear. I used a fancy font, as he requested. Then I printed a copy on faux-parchment stock, which made any words look good. It was pure magic. I read it over and my dad's line about "hearing Ted in the waves" gave me an idea for my letter. I retrieved it, adding a new paragraph:

```
When my own sister was nine years old,
and they took her for FGM, she died of an
infection caused by a rusty blade. I have
dedicated my work to her. I know she is
with me in spirit.
```

For the next half-hour, I wandered through Britannia until I heard Lisa's key in the lock. I switched back to my email program, hiding my tracks. A few minutes later, she came into the den and sat on the chair.

"We need to talk. We figured something out tonight about you and your dad."

"Whoa. You talk about my dad?"

"He still feels guilty because he couldn't save Ted so he closed his heart. He never gave you the love you needed. That's why you're always looking for it outside yourself. You want it, but you fear it. Just like me. It's not a coincidence that we were drawn to each other. We've got a chance now to break the pattern or repeat it again in another relationship, or another lifetime."

"Another lifetime?"

"Yes, another lifetime. Your dad's genetic code was written into your DNA, Murray. You soaked up all his beliefs and fears in the womb. You have the same longing for friendship that he does, and the same fear of opening your heart to take it on. Have you never wondered why you resent Brie so much? It's because you never really had a best friend. You know why? You're trying to be your dad's best friend. You're trying to replace Ted. And, my god, think of your dad's message today. You've done it. He thinks you're Ted."

"I've never heard such bullshit in all my life."

"They call that denial."

I turned away and went back to the computer, but she didn't let up. She walked around the edge of the desk to maintain eye contact.

"You told me once that your partner is your best friend. That's how it was with Paulette, Nicky and Cassandra. That's what you want with me. But you're afraid of intimacy. That's why your relationships never last." Her voice choked. "You glide along on the surface of life. That's why you spend so much time on the computer in your fantasy worlds. It's safer. You don't get hurt."

"Actually, I'm dead at the moment, and if you don't mind, I'd like to find a healer and get back in the game."

"I wish you would find a healer."

As she stood there, she saw my letter in the printer. She scanned it quickly, shaking her head in dismay.

"'A little off the top,' you said. You've completely butchered her words. Talk about mutilation."

"I did what needed to be done."

"I don't know who you are. You are so closed-hearted and mean-spirited. I think we need some time apart. I'm going to Indonesia after all. I've just decided."

"So go."

She said "Indonesia." I'm sure of it. But what I heard was "I don't need ya." She said other things too, between the wails, words I couldn't make out.

Games We Play

On the last Friday in August, exactly one month after Lisa's return from Indonesia, we were playing Boggle, a shake-the-letters-find-the-words kind of game. She searched for long words, which were more valuable. I scribbled down small words quickly. You only got points for seeing words the other couldn't see. When you found the same words, they cancelled each other out.

"This is it," she said. "I only need another twenty points. You are going to lose big."

Maybe so, but I would go out fighting. I raised the tray over my shoulder and shook like a gambler working dice. When it was Lisa's turn to shake, she always eased the letters into the tray with the least amount of noise.

"I think they're mixed."

And still I shook.

"Enough already."

I set the tray down, triumphant.

"Flip it," she said, pointing to the egg-timer, trying to save face.

While the sand slipped through the glass, we searched the jumbled letters for meaning. In the three minutes allotted, we would see different words. We always did.

"Time's up," I said.

"So what have you got?"

I gave the usual list of prepositions and three-letter words. Lisa saw "love."

"Maybe it's a sign," she said.

Since her trip, Lisa had been seeing "things that just happen" as "meaningful signs." She'd forged her own spiritual path—a blend of Buddhism, Wicca, the inner child theories of John Bradshaw, the music of the Indigo Girls and polarity therapy. On the inside, I was alternately mystified and envious about this new path. Outside, I supported her new spiritual-and-career directions. I played banker, writing post-dated cheques for the polarity therapy training she wanted to take in Montreal—a paternal arrangement that both soothed and irritated us.

Seeing "love" put Lisa over the top.

She turned the tray of letters over absently, watching "love" and all the other words disappear. I could almost hear the fears clattering in her head.

"It bothers me you didn't see 'love,'" she said.

"I didn't see 'dove' either."

"That's true."

She put the game to one side.

"Can we talk? I'm not happy with the way things are going."

"What things?"

"God, Murray," she said, starting to get up. I held her arm, and she allowed herself to be guided back down.

"We've been living together a year. I'm not the same person I was."

"You're coming out."

She shook her head. "You just can't accept that Brie and I can be close without being sexual."

"She has always tried to come between us, right from the start."

"Did it ever occur to you that if it wasn't for Brie, we wouldn't be together at all?"

I looked at her, baffled.

Lisa bowed her head, and then, with an extra effort, pulled up straight again.

"I've told you things, private things about Brie and me, to help you understand why we're so close. That brother of hers who locked her in the closet. She needed me, and I needed her, especially after my dad died. I trusted you enough to tell you those things."

"I know."

"Doesn't that count for anything?"

We were silent for a few moments.

"Yes. Sure it does."

"My relationship with Brie is changing too. I'm starting to see how we hold each other back. I've got to work some things out with her."

She paused, waiting for me to tell her what I was going to work out. I said nothing. I had been supposed to work on myself while she was travelling in Indonesia. I tried to read her self-help books. I kept falling asleep.

"We hold each other back too, Murray. I get wrapped up in your stuff because it lets me off the hook. I don't have to look at myself if I'm obsessing about you. Well, it's time to own your shit. Me and you both. You think you can do that?"

"Yes," I said. Because that was the right answer.

"Great. Let's start over with Brie too. She's invited us for a 'games' night tomorrow. She's got a new girlfriend. Sharon."

"What happened to Teresa?"

Lisa shrugged.

"Brie's working on a new performance piece," she said. "Maybe she'll do it for us."

Lisa looked at me, searching for a flicker of acknowledgment that watching Brie perform in that house was how we met.

"Just like old times then?" I said.

"Maybe we could just pretend that none of us had any history. That we really were starting over."

"Okay. Let's try."

I smiled warmly, but I couldn't keep up with her. First she wanted those moments of intimacy that can only come from shared history, then she wanted to throw it all away. What she really wanted, maybe, was to keep the good stuff, and toss out the crossed wires, the frictions, the icy silences. Was that actually possible, or were good and bad part of the same indivisible package? I met Stacy at the office looking for a summer job. She invited me to the house party. Brie was her roommate. Lisa was Brie's best friend. After Stacy interrupted my fight with her brother, I asked Lisa out to regain some dignity. Take any single element out of that big picture, and it all collapsed. I vowed to start over. This time, I would focus my attention lavishly and completely on Lisa. I would be content with her, and my eyes would not wander.

When we arrived at Brie's house, Sharon was already there. Nearly six feet tall, with black, shoulder-length hair, she towered above Brie. This, I thought, was one relationship going nowhere.

Once we'd got our drinks, and ordered the pizza, we settled into the living-room. Brie and Sharon sat in opposing chairs, while Lisa and I sat side-by-side on the soft couch. The room smelled of fresh dust, probably stirred up by the vacuum, and I felt a sneeze coming on. I fought it, toying with the cards for a board game called Lovers and Liars that had been set on the coffee table. A videocam sitting on a tripod at the other end of the room seemed aimed at me.

"How did you two meet?" I asked, for something to say.

"At SAW Video," Sharon said. "I've been helping with her new piece. Brie, you should really show some of the footage tonight. It's amazing."

"No, I don't think so. Not till it's finished." She shuffled the cards without looking up. Sharon rolled her eyes and pursed her lips. She glanced at me, mouthing the words, "lovers' quarrel."

"What's the video about?" I asked, looking at Sharon.

"It's called 'Out of the closet.'"

"Ah, I see. 'How I entered the sisterhood.'"

"Exactly," said Sharon, with a laugh.

Brie didn't respond to this exchange at her expense, but I saw a look pass between her and Lisa. I understood. It wasn't the "coming-out closet." It was the "locked closet."

"Let's get on with the show," Brie said. "Read the rules, Sharon. It's your game."

At that moment, Stacy popped her head in.

"You're just in time," Sharon said. "Come and play."

"No, I just wanted to say 'Hi.'"

"So say it," said Brie.

"She's been so charming these last few days, hasn't she, Sharon? I don't know if I could stand the pleasure of your company tonight, Brie."

"Why don't you take a cold shower then? Since no-one can stand your company either. Come back when you get the munchies."

Stacy's eyes watered, her lips parted slightly, but she managed to hold it together. She turned abruptly and headed upstairs.

"That was really mean," Sharon said. She looked at Lisa and me. "Stacy got dumped this week."

"And she's been sitting in her room, pouting and toking ever since. I'm running out of air freshener."

"Don't you remember what it's like to be dumped?" I said. "I thought you were the expert."

The doorbell rang.

"Pizza's here," said Lisa. "Can we call a truce everyone? This tension is giving me a headache. How do you play this game?"

As we carved up the pizza, Sharon gave an overview, but Brie interrupted. "Just tell them how you win. That's all Murray wants to know."

"Basically, it's about predicting whether the person will answer a question with a 'Yes,' 'No,' or 'Maybe,'" Sharon said. "You don't have to tell the truth."

"This should be right up your alley, Murray," Brie said.

I drew the first question, and turned to Lisa. "'Your lover says there's no need for you to work. I'll support you.' Do you accept the offer?'"

That's exactly what was happening now and I figured Lisa would tell the truth. I picked a "Yes" card from my pile and waited for Lisa to answer.

"Depends."

I placed my "Yes" card on the table, shrugging helplessly at Sharon.

"Remember, she doesn't have to tell the truth. Now Lisa, tell us why you said 'depends.'"

"It depends if I felt my lover was doing it for me or for him."

"Good answer. Take a new question and a new answer card, Murray."

I took another swig of hard lemonade.

"This will be a good game for you and Lisa," Brie said. "It'll help you get to know each other."

"Lay off," Lisa said.

Sharon went next, and turned to me.

"'You hit it off with someone at a party. Your lover seems jealous. Do you cut your conversation short?'"

"No."

"That's what I thought," she said, revealing a 'No' card.

"She's got your number," Brie said, putting on a brave face. She tore a slice off the pizza, and took a mouthful of beer to wash it down.

As the game progressed, Lisa had an uncanny ability to predict what Brie and I would say, even when we were second-guessing ourselves. She won easily. Brie came second, Sharon third. I was last.

"I'll be back in a minute," Lisa said, getting up.

"You have to jiggle the doorknob," Brie said.

"You're such a mind reader."

Sharon got up to get refills for everyone. I took a quick look at her butt as she walked by.

"Nice jiggle, eh?" Brie said. "I've been trying to think what it is women see in you. I think it's that Hugh Grant thing. Outwardly smooth and sensitive, inwardly superficial. Eventually people figure it out. How's it going with Lisa, anyway? I hear you're down to weeks, if not days."

"You're one to talk. How is it you have a new girlfriend every time we see you?"

Sharon and Lisa came back, and I got up.

"My turn."

"The little boy's room is up the stairs and at the end of the hall. Remember to lift the seat and put it back again," said Brie.

I refused to let Brie get to me. I left the living-room quickly and headed up the stairs. Stacy's door was slightly ajar, and I got a whiff of pot. The bathroom was steamy from the hot shower. After I zipped up, I left the seat up. I turned the doorknob, but it spun around and around. Then it opened from the other side: it was Stacy, standing there in a robe with a towel around her shoulders.

"We've been calling the landlord about that knob all week. I'm always rescuing people."

"Thanks."

"That's all I get?"

She turned her cheek out for a kiss. I pressed my lips against her still-wet skin.

"You want to join me for a quick toke?"

"Sure."

I thought I deserved some positive female attention. Stacy had the smallest room in the house—just enough space for a bed, a desk, a short chest of drawers and a small nightstand. We sat side-by-side on the narrow bed. She reached across my chest, pressing her breasts against me, to get the joint out of the ashtray. She took a deep drag, then handed it to me.

"I've always regretted inviting you to that party, where you met Lisa. I had designs on you." She grasped my shoulders, turning me to face her.

"Blow into me. You know you want to."

She pressed her mouth around my closed lips. I took care not to break the seal, then exhaled down her throat. She took it until she gagged. As she coughed, she blew second-hand smoke and saliva into my face. I coughed back. There was no escape from the smoke, the taste of pot, our body fluids, the panic in my heart. Then I heard spray from an aerosol can. A waft of pine scent entered Stacy's room.

"You've gotta love a girl on the rebound, eh Murray?"

Brie stood at the door, the videocam in her hands. She left, shutting the door behind her. The air freshener hung in the air, and then dissipated.

"Fucking bitch," Stacy said.

"She set you up for this, didn't she? This was all part of her master plan. Just like the way you set your brother on me at the party."

Stacy's tears flashed to anger. She pounded my chest with her fists.

"I should've let my brother beat the shit out of you."

I closed the door behind me. I stood in the hallway, trying to think myself out of this mess. I heard the toilet flush, and then the handle jiggle.

"Stacy!" Brie called out. "I'm locked in again. Please let me out."

Silence.

"Please. I'm sorry. I'll give you the tape."

More silence, except for the sound of the doorknob spinning round and round.

"Look, just let me out." She pounded against the door.

"Lisa! Help me. I need you!"

She was shouting now, and I heard the fear in her voice. I remembered her brother and the locked closet. Stacy hadn't stirred, and Lisa probably couldn't hear the shout over the music in the living-room. I could have bargained for the tape, but I simply turned the knob to let her out. I thought I would win some points just for rescuing her. But when she saw me, her eyes flashed hate. She pushed by me and headed downstairs.

By the time I reached the living-room, Brie was connecting the videocam to the television. I sat down, stone-faced, and reached for a new bottle of hard lemonade.

"She's going to show us some footage after all," Sharon said.

Brie sat down with the remote in her lap. "Let's have another game first," she said.

"It's late, Brie. We should really get going," Lisa said.

"Come on. The night is young. Let's just have a quick round without the cards. Murray, let's say you're in a relationship. You're at a party. You head upstairs for a piss when this gorgeous chick invites you into her room. She offers you a toke. She starts giving you mouth-to-mouth. Would you fuck her, if you could get away with it?"

I sat there, staring into space.

"I don't know what you saw, Brie, but just leave it alone," Lisa said.

"Come on, Murray. What do you say? Would you?"

"No."

"I doubt that." She started moving toward the television.

"Okay, Brie," I said. "Let's say you're a dyke, and you're in love with your best friend, who's straight. Do you try to convert her or let her get on with her life?"

"Depends if she's attracted to an asshole or not."

"Brie!" Sharon said. She turned to Lisa. "Can't you make them stop?"

"No, let them go at it. Let's get this over with."

"How many women have you messed up?" Brie held up a pretend mirror. "I see Cassandra and Nicky. And Paulette. And Lisa. Oh, and there's Stacy too. Do you have to hit on every woman you see just to know you're alive?"

I imagined every intimate detail of my life passing between Lisa and Brie. I walked over to Brie, using my height to tower over her. "Do you screw your way through high school, and then decide it's easier to come out than make peace with your messed-up family? I mean, why didn't your brother just keep you in the closet?"

Brie laughed in a giddy, uncontrolled way. She sank to her knees, and bent over to hide her face. Her laughter quickly turned to sobs. I stood there, arms folded tightly against my chest, wishing I could take back the words. Lisa walked over to Brie.

"I'm sorry. I should never have told him."

Brie held out her arms, but Lisa just squeezed both of Brie's hands. She took a step back.

"I can't protect you anymore," Lisa said. "You need to feel it now."

"Feel it. You don't think I feel it every day. Miss Fucking Self-Help. What do you know?"

She pushed at Lisa, but she had no strength. She crawled into a corner and threw up. Lisa sat in a corner against a wall. I went to her, but she pushed me away.

"This is my shit. Go deal with your own. On your own."

I felt abandoned and ashamed, angry and hurt, conciliatory and defiant. The emotions cancelled each other out.

Closing Up

Dad calls me straight, without the one-ring signal. Mom's got pneumonia, but there might be more to it. She can't hold food down. They're doing some more tests.

"We're stuck here awhile."

It's late October and they've usually closed up the cottage and left for Florida by now. Mom's illness has put them behind schedule and Dad's worried about the water system.

"Any day now, the frost could hit and wreck the pipes. It'll be a hell of a mess."

He talks louder to combat the sound of a TV news-report on the sinking of a ferry in Bangladesh. I'm watching it too. I half listen through the telephone because I've muted the sound on my set.

"There's been a hell of an accident in some country," he says. "Jesus."

"I heard. Terrible."

"It's just like the war, when we got hit by the torpedo. Ted was down below, you know. He couldn't get out. I tried, though. I really did."

Silence.

"I've got some deadlines at work so I won't be able to leave Ottawa until Saturday morning."

"Just don't expect a lot when you get here. I've been living on soup and sandwiches."

Silence.

"Paulette will be coming," he says. A statement more than a question. He's confusing Paulette with Lisa, and he's forgotten that Lisa's moved out, but he says the words with such authority, I almost believe one of them is still in my life.

"No, Dad. Just me."

"All right then," he says, and we hang up.

It bothers me to hear my father so detached from my mother's illness, unwilling to face this harsh truth. Lisa would probably say I'm aiding and abetting his denial by not confronting him or reaching out. The time has come to break us out of our patterns. I will be compassionate and caring, but challenging too. If she were only here, Lisa would be so proud.

A month ago, on the morning Lisa moved out, we stood awkwardly at the door. I kept thinking about how sad I would be in a few moments, how I would wander through the apartment, noting the space on the bookshelves, listening for the last echo of the hangers clanging together in the closet.

"You're off somewhere again, aren't you?"

"Sorry."

"Yeah, I know you are." Her voice wasn't sarcastic or hurt, just defeated.

She hugged me, and then turned away quickly. Afterwards, my self-guided tour didn't turn out. With nothing to prop them up, my books had simply collapsed on most of the shelves. In the bedroom closet, the hangers were still. She had left a bag of old clothes that no longer fit just inside the door, ready for Neighbourhood Services. In the bathroom, I checked for forgotten toiletries, but it was bare and her scent was already disappearing. In the kitchen, the freezer was empty except for a plastic tray of dehydrated ice cubes.

As I looked at Lisa's boxes, piled against the wall or pushed off to one side, I tried to catch sight of the numbers and remember what was inside. I poured a glass of Lisa's ginger ale. It was flat. I dropped in three slivers of ice and sat on the sofa, feet up on box number eight, waiting for something to happen. It didn't so I added rye.

I had gallantly and stupidly offered to keep Lisa's boxes for a few months until she got settled. She was moving to Montreal to pursue polarity therapy. She would live with her sister. It was a chance for them to work stuff out, she said. Everything was an opportunity for personal growth for Lisa. I admired her for that, but resented she had grown out of me.

Of course, she had grown out of Brie, too. That should have been some comfort, but it wasn't. My goal had been to vanquish Brie, saving Lisa from a life of lesbianism, and then live happily ever after with Lisa. It never occurred to me that by defeating her best friend, I could defeat myself as well. The three of us were bound up in a single package. Why did it matter so much? Because I'd lost.

After a week of tripping over Lisa's boxes in the living-room, I moved them all into the den, lining them up against the wall like blocks of ice. Even when I wasn't working in the den, I sensed the boxes there. I kept waiting for spring to melt them away. But it was autumn, and like my dad said, it was just getting colder. In my place, the frost had already hit. I was stuck with her boxes, but just as I had done for Paulette, Nicky and Cassandra, I decided to box up reminders of Lisa—the notes and cards, the photos and mementos—and store them at the cottage in a cryogenics experiment. Years later, when my heart had sufficiently evolved, I would thaw out the contents, letting the old feelings of love spring back to life and wash over me.

With Lisa's box in the passenger seat, I drive straight to the hospital on Saturday morning. At first, I think I've got the wrong room. I don't recognize the figure sleeping in bed, hooked up to tubes. It's the hair, all frizzy and grey. I've never seen it uncombed before and without black dye.

Dad said they put her in chronic care because there were no more beds at the Brockville General, where people get better. Now that I see my mother, I wonder if there's another reason. I leave my Get Well Soon card on the tray and slip out again.

When I pull into the cottage, Dad is crouched over the step, looking for something. He stands up as I approach. We hug and he holds me longer than usual, the weight of his body pressing into mine.

"I saw her," I say, breaking the embrace. "She was sleeping."

"How did she look?"

"Not too bad."

"We'll go back after lunch. Right now, I'm looking for the key to Bonnie's garage."

Bonnie was an elderly neighbour up the road who let us use her garage. In return, Dad cut her lawn and oiled the road in front of her place to keep the dust down.

"Where have you been today?"

"Christ, I've been down to the hospital. I've been to the garage. I've been down to the pumphouse. I was in the water fixing the boat rack. It could be anywhere. It's probably on the bottom of the river. It's your mother's fault. She doesn't sew up my pockets."

"I'm sure it'll turn up."

But in my mind I see Dad walking too fast, slightly stooped, his torso leaning ahead of his legs. The key could have fallen out while he was pounding down the fire-escape steps to the dock. He wouldn't have heard it hit the metal rungs or seen it slip through to the earth underneath. Or maybe he stumbled along the path that led to the pump-house. The key could have dropped fifteen feet into the water below or sunk into the rotting leaves under the cliff. It really could be anywhere.

"What's so important to get out of the garage?"

"Letters from Ted. Before we joined the navy, he spent some time out west. He wrote me these letters."

"I'm sure they'll turn up."

I follow him into the cottage. The shutters are already on the windows so it takes a moment for my eyes to adjust to the darkness. Then he flicks on a light and I have to adjust all over again.

As I put my bag in the room, I see Dad has laid out two open suitcases on my bed. They're empty, waiting for Mom's return. He's not sure what they bring to Florida. I close them up for now and put them to one side.

Dad pops some bread in the toaster and breaks out the

bananas and peanut butter. Afterwards, we stack our plates and soup bowls with the others sitting beside the sink.

When we see Mom, she's awake and I peck her on the cheek.

"You should eat something," Dad says, waving at the untouched food on her tray. "You'll never get better."

Her face tightens and shakes.

"I'm trying." She motions for water. I refill the glass and place it in her hands.

"Murray and I are eating well, aren't we son?"

Mom frowns.

"Did that specialist come by yet?" he asks.

"They took more blood this morning. They won't know anything until next week."

"Jesus. I'm going to find that doctor who was here yesterday."

When Dad leaves, I sit in one of the guest chairs.

"You haven't opened your card."

"Thank you," she says, after reading the canned sentiment.

Dad comes back, muttering about the doctor who doesn't work Saturdays. He complains for a few more minutes until Mom has to pee. I slip into the empty TV-room next door, leaving him to help her get onto the chair. There's an old war-movie playing and I curl up on the sofa, trying to get comfortable.

When Lisa and I watched TV, she would lie against one end of the sofa with her knees up, and I would rest my back against her. We would tape mysteries and watch them at our own speed.

"Pause," she would say, and as the image was frozen on the screen, we would trade theories about the killer. "He's too obvious," she'd say. Or after the detective stumbled onto an important clue, I would say: "Okay, now what does that mean?"

On quiet nights, alone on the sofa at home, I can almost

hear Lisa behind me, analyzing why so-and-so was murdered, or dissecting why our relationship was falling apart.

Dad pops his head into the TV-room in the middle of an attack on a German battleship. He looks at the screen and shakes his head.

"I wish to hell I could find those letters. Your mother needs to sleep. We'll come back after dinner."

I follow Dad to her room, kiss her goodbye and shut the blinds to block out the afternoon sun.

"My eyes have been bothering me," Dad says, during the drive home. "It's not bad now. But at night, I see lights all over the place. I had them checked last week, but he didn't find anything wrong."

"Maybe I should drive tonight."

"No, it's not that bad. I can manage."

When we arrive at the cottage, Dad has the itinerary planned. As we rake, he talks about wills and safety-deposit boxes. By the time we've pushed the leaves onto a tarpaulin and dumped them over the cliff, he's moved on to probate fees and power of attorney. We're chopping firewood when he starts on about cremation, how it's the cheapest way to dispose of a dead body.

"If we go in Florida, don't bring us back. Just be done with it there."

Neither of us suggest Mom may not make it to Florida.

"I could drive you to Florida."

"There's no need for that."

"You'll be tired by the time you're ready to go."

"We'll see."

I drop the idea for now, but stay poised to bring it up again.

Down at the dock, we cover the cockpit of the sailboat with plywood so the tarp won't sag down into the hole from the weight of water or ice.

"Ted and I had so much fun on the water. I wrote a poem

about how I can still hear him in the waves. I've sent it to a contest. I think I've got a good chance of winning. It's not like you're writing about a bird. This is real human interest. I sent them a photo of us together."

I don't remind him I typed the poem. Nor do I tell him they'll simply toss the photograph in the garbage. As he wipes away tears, I pretend not to notice. I just look out at the river, remembering the times I took my lovers sailing. I can see Nicky pressed against me as we beat up wind; Paulette ducking under the boom as we tack; Lisa laughing with excitement as the centreboard hums on a beam reach; Cassandra lying on the bow, the mast between her legs, as we head home on a dead run.

When the chores are done, we throw wood on the fire and take a short nap.

Around 6.30, we head downtown for a pizza and then visit the hospital again. Dad drives.

She's asleep when we look in. We stand at the door for a few moments, uncertain, then decide to leave. Dad finds a night nurse.

"She should be getting better by now," he says.

"These things take time."

We tell her to tell Mom we stopped in, then pick up a video and drive home.

"You see that car over there. See, when I squint, it's like a transport truck, all lit up. Jesus. There, right there. There are so many lights."

"I really think I should drive you to Florida."

"Maybe you're right."

I hold my breath, not daring to believe I've really convinced him.

I'm lying in bed, listening to Dad's voice on the other side of the wall. With the shutter on the window, it's absolutely dark in my bedroom. It could be the middle of the night or early morning. In a monotone, Dad is reading to someone, describing Mom's symptoms and the attempts at treatment. I think the worst, I always do. When he opens my door, I blink from the light. A sound leaves my throat.

"Are you laughing or crying?"

I don't answer, but hold out my arms like a child. His body envelops mine and this time I don't pull back.

"I heard you talking."

More tears now, from both of us.

"I was talking to a doctor. They put her on a different drug yesterday. I don't know what's going to happen."

At first, our voices waver and crack in the semi-darkness. After a few seconds, the broken spaces and silences are filled. Fully awake now, I let my arms fall and the moment passes.

The new medication seems to be working because Mom is looking better on Sunday. She dictates a list of clothes to pack and Dad happily writes it all down. In the car, on the way back to the cottage, he taps out a rhythm on the steering wheel.

"We should be gone by the end of the week."

"I can still drive you."

"There's no need for that. Your mother is fine now."

"But she doesn't drive anyway. You do all the driving."

"We'll be fine."

"You're still blinking."

"What's that?"

I raise my voice: "You need to turn your left indicator off."

"Right."

He clicks it off, ending the discussion.

With Mom on the mend, and Dad starting to pack up the clothes, I decide it's time to head home. Then, in the bathroom, I spot the key to Bonnie's garage on the rug near the space heater.

"Found it."

"Well for god's sake. Let's take a look."

I should be relieved he's no longer so anxious to find the letters, but instead I'm disappointed he's not more excited. Dad waits for me to get the box from my car. We walk up the road together.

"I'm sure I've told you how he saved my life. We were walking across the river in the middle of winter. The ice gave way and I fell in. Ted pulled me out. I wish I could have pulled him out when we were hit by the torpedo. I tried, but I just couldn't get back to him."

"You did your best."

Dad doesn't respond. Either he didn't hear me or he doesn't believe me.

Bonnie's garage has two doors that come together in the middle. One of them sticks in the earth and has to be lifted slightly, while the other is too high and wants to swing shut. When I look inside, blinking in the dim light, I smell sawdust and something dead. Probably a squirrel. They slip in when the door's open and get trapped. Dad doesn't acknowledge the stench so neither do I.

The garage is jam-packed with our rowboat, an old tablesaw, a lawnmower and a few dozen boxes stacked on shelves or up from the dirt floor on bricks. I place Lisa's box in the rowboat, nestling it between two waterlogged life-preservers. Then we start opening boxes, using a trouble-light to flash into the darker corners. It's all junk: old dishes, picture frames, broken appliances, magazines and Reader's Digest condensed books. After a half hour, with just a handful of boxes left on a small shelf over the rowboat, I can sense hope beginning to fade. We pull each down in turn, but one large box is tucked at the end, just out of reach.

"You want to bother?" I ask, knowing the answer.

"That'll be the one they're in. Just you wait."

I look around and find a wooden stepladder. We have to make space on the floor for its feet, but even then there isn't much room.

"I'll go up," I say.

"All right. But there's a rung missing so be careful. And watch out for nails in the beams up there."

I take the trouble-light with me, and climb up slowly. I see a couple of sharp points sticking out of the rafters, rusted dark brown from humidity. I keep my head bent slightly, struggling to breathe. The air is close up there and it makes my chest heavy.

"Just open it up there. Don't try to bring it down."

I find a hook in one of the rafters for the trouble-light, freeing my hands to open the flaps. I half expect to find a dead animal inside. Instead, I see piles of old games, packed up after Nicky left and Paulette showed no interest. I pull them out one by one to see what's underneath. Cootie is on top, followed by Monopoly, Stock Ticker, Masterpiece and Battleship. At the very bottom, I pull up a handful of plastic ice-blocks from Don't Break the Ice. The little man you try to keep from falling through the ice is nowhere in sight.

"Anything?"

"Nothing."

I close it up again, then start down with the light. I forget about the missing rung, lose my balance and drop the last yard to the ground. I land on my feet and Dad grabs me before I fall over.

"I've got you."

In the close quarters of the garage, surrounded by the stench of death, he hugs me until I can hardly breathe. It's not really me he's hugging, but I let him do it anyway.

Planned Giving

Hello Murray,

I am writing to you from Whole Women in Talime, where I met today with Rhobi Juba. I am just heading home, but wanted to send you good news while I have access to email. (Our system in Dar has been down for several days.) As I told you, Rhobi was distressed to see how you had rewritten her letter for the fundraising campaign on female genital mutilation. I decided to visit in person to explain, as best I could, that the Ottawa staff knows the audience for these letters better than we do in Tanzania. We had to stretch the truth of her actual experience to make it seem more truthful. It is a contradiction she finally understood. So this rift is healed, and she is grateful she has helped Friends of Africa raise money. She has also agreed to write diary excerpts of her FGM work with the young girls for the website. Everything has gone well.

I must go now. It's getting late, and you know these roads.

My best to you, my friend.

Frank

Everything was indeed going well. Our FGM campaign had surpassed all expectations, leaving Friends of Africa *en route* to reach its fundraising target a month before the end of our fiscal year. Rhobi Juba's diary excerpts—carefully shaped by me, of course—would give all those donors the warm and fuzzies, and keep them coming back to our website for feel-good reports of their money in action. After the diaries got them all stirred up, our loyal readers would be predisposed to click our new online donation button to keep the good feelings—and the cash—flowing. And this afternoon, David and I would kickstart our planned-giving program by signing up a rich widow eager to leave a legacy of health through us in her will.

If I had any regrets, it was Lisa's absence. She had been so critical of my decision to rewrite Rhobi's original letter. It would have been sweet to show her Frank's email to prove I was right. Apart from that, I didn't really miss Lisa. Our time together had reached its natural end. I did struggle through Christmas and New Year's on my own, but Valentine's Day was over, and spring would soon arrive—the season of waist-high jackets and tight jeans. As Frank once said to me, there's always another fish in the sea.

In fact, I was ready to reel in a young woman named Nancy Sheffield. On the telephone, she sounded young and perky, but with a cynical edge, probably from having spent the last two years with CUSO in Nigeria. She wanted to talk about volunteering with Friends of Africa—code words for, "I've been out of the country and I need a job." When she mentioned her plan to skate here, I had suggested an 11.30 meeting. Then I brought my own skates, planting them in full sight of the visitor's chair. If she were attractive, it would be easy to skate with her during lunch, and go for a hot chocolate. It was so damned cold out today we'd have to stick close together on the ice. After that, anything could happen.

After I popped into the kitchen for coffee, I had two messages waiting on voicemail. In the first, Nancy cancelled our meeting with a lame excuse about having found a job. In the second, my father announced he'd taken a silver in the poetry contest for his "Ode to Ted." He then read the poem, forgetting I had typed it up for him. Mercifully, the system cut him off just after he'd read the lines, "Although you left us years ago, a life I could not save/on still clear mornings, I yet hear your voice upon the waves." But even if he didn't reach the grand finale, I still heard the rhymes in my head: "And though you drowned alone that day in that terrible, terrible war/I will hold your memory dear, today and forever more."

Zap. Message deleted. If only Dad could do that to his

memory banks, we'd all be a lot happier. It occurred to me then that he didn't want to let Ted go. That was the difference between us: I was more than willing to leave friends and lovers behind. Cassandra, Nicky, Paulette and now Lisa. Someone else would come along. They always did. If not today, then tomorrow, and forever more.

Just before noon, David stopped by my office, dressed to kill as usual. Apart from David and the executive director, none of the men at Friends of Africa wore suits unless we had a Board meeting or an interview for another job. I had put mine on today for our meeting with Mrs. McMaster, and it made me feel like I was halfway out the door.

"Bad news," David said, pausing. "Hank Chande died yesterday. He was out of town, coming home late. Someone was driving on the wrong side of the road without headlights. I thought you'd want to know."

David pursed his lips, fiddled with his tie, and nodded solemnly.

"His name was Frank," I said. But David didn't hear me. He had already turned, and the clatter of his leather shoes on the floor drowned out my words.

I walked to the canal, leaving my skates behind. I found a bench on the path above the canal, brushed off the snow, plunked myself down and stared at the postcard scene unfolding below on the ice. Workers on lunch-break mixed with Moms and their preschoolers, old folks and lovers. I remembered taking a photo of Frank standing on the canal, and then seeing it on his bookshelf in Dar es Salaam. It stood next to one of his two sons—Charles, who drowned, and John, who watched it happen, unable to help. The photo was supposed to show John that water was safe, even frozen water. When I went for dinner with Frank and his wife Halima, and I saw John's blank face, I didn't think Frank's plan had worked. What would John think now? Water and roads—neither were safe. I remembered driving back from Talime last fall with Frank when an oncoming car forced us onto the shoulder. Then I told myself if I had gone with Rhobi Juba's original letter, he wouldn't have driven back to see her. He would still be alive. None of this was helping me feel better so I got up and walked quickly back to the office, as if speed alone would distance me from my dark thoughts.

Helen McMaster lived on Clemow Avenue in the Glebe, easily one of the most expensive strips of residential real estate in Ottawa. It was only proper, then, that David should drive us there in his Dodge Viper. Flashy cars and finely tailored suits were holdovers from his days as a high-flying advertising executive in Toronto. He was in his mid fifties, financially secure and trying now—as he so often told me—to do some good in the world. But no-one said he couldn't do good in style.

"I really shouldn't be driving this in the winter with all the salt," he said, as we settled inside. "But what the hell. Life is short. And we want to make a good impression."

As I buckled in, the smell of suede and leather enveloped me. I watched him slip his manicured hands into driving gloves that matched the dark tone of the steering wheel, which in turn, complemented his hard-shell briefcase. Last year, I had finally broken down and bought a soft leather briefcase. It had a strap so I could easily sling it over my shoulder if I rode my bicycle to work. But the knapsack still worked better so I scrunched the briefcase in my office closet, pulling it out for important meetings outside the office. I sat now in my suit with the wrinkled briefcase in my lap, feeling out of place.

"When we get there, let me do the talking," David said. "If for any reason, I want you to intervene, I'll tap your shoe."

Out of impatience and boredom, David always did the talking. He had no real interest in hearing about the latest returns from a direct-mail package, or how many donations the 1-800 number had brought in. He liked big ideas—like planned giving. Once the ideas were in motion, he moved on. I wondered how much longer he would last at Friends of Africa. We only had so much money for big ideas.

David pulled into the driveway of a two-storey stone house behind a black BMW sedan.

"These don't come cheap," he said. "I think we've hit pay dirt."

"It's not exactly an old lady's car."

"It's in the driveway. That's what's important."

I had left my boots at the office, putting on well-worn galoshes over my good shoes. With the lack of tread, I slipped as I reached the step, nearly toppling over. It reminded me of Frank Chande again, how I had let him fall on the canal while I was staring at a mystery woman tying her skates on a bench. The canal was not far from Clemow, and I longed to walk on the path above it, watching closely for women to rescue.

"This is it. Look sharp," David said. He rang the bell, and the deep tones that rang forth sounded from some other time.

An attractive woman in her early forties wearing a wool sweater and jeans answered the door.

"Good afternoon," David said, sticking out his hand. "I'm David Spencer from Friends of Africa."

I felt a flash of embarrassment at the slick sound of David's voice. We were door-to-door salesmen, peddling legacies.

She took his hand, but looked at me. A corner of her lip turned up ever so slightly. It was a look my old girlfriend Nicky would give when faced with some aspect of contemporary culture that cried out for irony.

"And you are?" she said.

"Murray Lockhart. The sidekick."

She laughed. "My name is Alicia. I believe you're here to see my aunt."

"Yes, that's right," David said, quickly, but Alicia had already turned back into the doorway. He stuck out his arm, blocking me so he could follow her first. When we took off our coats, Alicia held out her arms to receive mine, not his.

The brush of her fingers on my hand said, "possibility." After she left us in the living-room to find her aunt, David gave me a stern look.

"We're here to win over the aunt, not the niece. Keep your mind on the job."

I started to speak, but he shook his head, cutting me off. "Don't talk. Listen. And learn."

I gave him my own hard look, then turned away. My eyes strayed to the photographs on the mantel. A series of tiny daguerreotypes in gold frames gave way to black and white photos of a World War II pilot beside his plane and a war-time wedding photo: a dashing young officer grinning beside his shy bride. At the far end, in an eight-by-ten graduation portrait, Alicia stared back with a faraway look that undressed me. I wanted a wallet-size version. Even an unfinished proof would do.

"Oh, Alicia, you should have told them to sit down."

I turned to see Mrs. McMaster shuffle into the room behind a walker with Alicia following a few steps behind. Even with her wrinkled face and white hair, I could see the young woman from the wedding photo. After she helped lower her aunt into a plush chair, Alicia disappeared into the kitchen for a pot of tea. David and I took places on the settee. I could almost hear him calculating how many months the old lady had left.

"It's so nice of you to visit," she said.

"Not at all, not at all," David said. "When you contacted us about our programs...."

"I really want to leave a legacy on behalf of my husband, Richard. There he is beside the Spitfire," she said, pointing to the mantel. David and I looked over our shoulders politely.

"He was shot down in North Africa, and some of the local children saved his life. He always wanted to repay them. So I thought what better way than to give them the gift of health."

David smiled, but said nothing. Maybe he didn't know we

only worked in African countries south of the Sahara, and that Mrs. McMaster's gift would never fulfill her late husband's wishes. But I did, and I kept my mouth shut.

"Alicia, there you are. Let it steep a few moments before you pour."

"The wonderful thing about our planned-giving program is that you're able to create a legacy in your husband's name. You can arrange regular payments now or through your will. We also hope that you'll allow us to tell Mr. McMaster's story. It deserves to be heard so other people can be inspired. We would write it up in our newsletter."

"My husband always wanted to be a writer," she said, dreamily. "He wrote me marvellous letters from England during the war."

"Maybe we could take excerpts from some of those letters for the article," I said. "I'm the writer at Friends of Africa, and I would be happy to do that."

David leaned forward to put his teacup back on the coffee table. As he did, he gave me a light tap with his shoe—a nod of approval for my well-timed intervention.

"I guess that's why they call you the sidekick," Alicia said.

"What's that dear?"

"Nothing, Aunt Helen. I was just admiring Mr. Spencer's shoes."

"His shoes?"

"It doesn't matter."

"Well," David began, brightly, as if nothing had happened.

"Do you write the direct-mail letters too?" Alicia said, looking at me. She kept her face neutral, but I sensed she knew the answer already, and was trying to trip me up. There was no shame in admitting I wrote the letters that went out in other people's names, but it felt like giving away a trade secret.

"I oversee them," I said.

"We were very impressed with the letter from the woman

in Tanzania a few months back, weren't we, Aunt Helen? It was so well-written."

This time, Alicia's bemused tone was not—as we said at Friends of Africa—inclusive. She was taunting me to come clean. I wondered how Helen McMaster had seen the FGM package in the first place. Old widows didn't exactly fit our target demographic of professional urban women. Maybe Alicia had received it at her home, and shared it with her aunt. I looked at Alicia's skeptical face. I wanted to know where she lived so I could check her postal code. Then I remembered Frank Chande explaining how they got along in Dar es Salaam without a street address. "If someone doesn't know our house, they ask for directions," he'd said. I could see me and David wandering the streets of Dar for hours, two white guys in suits, searching in vain for Frank's house so we could give Halima some flowers and sign her up for planned giving. No-one would help us, and I couldn't blame them.

"Murray may have given her a few tips," said David, chuckling. "But we make sure we involve our beneficiaries in everything we do."

Our partners, I wanted to say. We fund the partners. The partners help the beneficiaries.

"So your husband liked to write, Mrs McMaster. What did he do for a living?" David's smooth delivery didn't quite mask his growing frustration with our meandering conversation.

"He was in the insurance business. He liked to help people. He was volunteering for Meals on Wheels last year when he had the accident. They think he hit the gas instead of the brake. It was a godsend no-one else was hurt."

"Driving can be dangerous, especially in the developing world," said David. "Just this morning we got news that our field officer in Tanzania, Hank Chande, was killed in a car accident yesterday."

I tensed up at the wrong name, and then watched David's shameless strategy to exploit Frank's death work its magic:

Mrs. McMaster pulled a tissue from inside her sleeve and dabbed her eyes. I wanted to expose David as a fraud artist who would sell his soul for money, but I couldn't do it without exposing myself as well.

"He was married, I suppose."

"I believe so."

"Such a sad thing, to be widowed in that way. At least Richard and I had many years together, and a full life. I do hope he had some kind of insurance policy."

"I'm not sure, but Friends of Africa provides generous survivor benefits. She'll be well taken care of."

My teeth hurt from the clenching. If she were lucky, Halima would maintain her modest lifestyle for a few years. When the death benefits ran their course, her standard of living would plunge. As I sat there, drinking tea from fine china, the whole idea of someone with enough money to give it away felt grotesque.

"Hank worked very hard for us," David said. "He was involved with a project to protect young girls from mutilation. That was the project highlighted in the letter you were speaking about a few moments ago. We hope to publish diary excerpts on our website so you can follow the project along, and see how your money is being spent."

"Oh, I don't know anything about that web business," said Mrs. McMaster. She blushed, shook her head, and looked away.

"Don't worry. We'll also print them in the donor newsletter that we mail out."

David, you're an idiot, I thought. She doesn't care about the website; she's embarrassed that you mentioned FGM.

"We'll look forward to reading her diaries," said Alicia. "The woman is such a good writer. But speaking of the Internet, I couldn't find any reference to North Africa on your website."

David took a sip of tea to buy time.

"We're often so busy that we fall behind on updating the

site," he said, reaching for his briefcase. "And I'm sure you're busy too, and I don't want to keep you two all afternoon. I've brought some forms I'd like to show you. You'll want to review these with your lawyer."

"That would be me," Alicia said, taking the package. "I'll put these with the others."

"Others?"

"We've been meeting with different aid groups to evaluate their planned-giving programs. My aunt plans to make a generous gift, and we want to make sure it will reflect my uncle's wishes. I hope you weren't expecting a cheque today."

"Of course not."

David snapped his briefcase shut again.

"Well," he said. "Do you have any questions we can answer?"

"We'll let you know," Alicia said.

I glanced at Mrs. McMaster, who seemed lost in thought. Then I realized she was staring at the photograph of her husband behind me.

"My father was in the war," I said. "In the navy."

"Was he?" Mrs. McMaster brightened.

I had really only wanted to connect with her in some way, but David and Alicia saw it differently. David smiled, pleased that I had kept us in the game. Alicia stared at me coldly for the same reason.

"Where was he stationed?"

"Mostly in Norway. He lost his best friend there. They were torpedoed."

"Oh dear. Richard lost good friends too."

"Your father wasn't stationed in North Africa, then?" Alicia said. Her faraway look in the photograph was long gone. Her sarcasm was so close I could almost see the frost on her breath.

I shook my head.

"But Murray has been to Africa," said David, brightly. "He met with Hank Chande to learn more about our projects, and to be able to tell our donors how their money is helping give children the gift of health." He squeezed my shoulder with faux-affection.

All I had to do was smile at Mrs. McMaster, feed her another line that would open her heart and make her push aside her niece's skepticism. When it came time to decide on a planned-giving program, she would remember the nice young man whose father fought in the war, and how the father's friend had died at sea, and how the African man had died in the car accident, and this would evoke bittersweet memories of her dead husband, and she would give willingly to Friends of Africa to keep those memories alive. I saw this all so clearly in her face.

"His name was Frank," I said. "It was not Hank. It was Frank."

"It's all right, Murray," David said, patting my knee. "I know it's difficult. Murray and Frank were very close. His death was so unexpected. But we never know when death will come for us, do we? That's why it's important to plan ahead."

"Enough!" I said, pushing his hand away. "Will you stop this bullshit?"

I got up quickly, knocking the coffee table and spilling tea out of my cup onto the saucer.

I moved toward Mrs. McMaster.

"There's something I need to tell you," I said. "I know it's important for you that your husband's gift go to the right children. I'm sorry to say that Friends of Africa doesn't work in North Africa."

Her eyes watered at my words, and a shadow of disappointment crept across her face. I held her gaze. After all the subterfuge, I owed her that much.

"What Murray means," David began.

"I think it's pretty clear what he means," Alicia said, getting up.

"Yes, well, as I said, this death has hit Murray very hard. He's not himself."

"So who the hell am I, then?" I shouted the words, and my voice cracked.

There was an awkward silence, as if we were all waiting for an answer. Then David, true to form, tried to salvage the moment.

"Who are any of us?" he said. "Where do we come from? And where are we going? Maybe we're all part of a larger whole. Canada. South Africa. North Africa. East Africa. Maybe, in the end, it doesn't matter."

I looked at him, and started to laugh.

"We should go, Murray, and let these young ladies get on with their day."

"Did you ever hear such bullshit?" I said to Alicia.

"Only in court."

David shook hands with Mrs. McMaster, and then walked briskly toward the hall. He put on his boots and coat.

"Are you coming, Murray?"

"No."

"A word then, please."

I walked over. He started to speak, but I cut him off.

"Before you fire me, I quit."

"After what you've done here, I'll make sure you never work in this field again," he said, hissing out the words.

"You'll be doing me a favour."

A few moments later, he shut the door behind him. As I took my coat off the rack, Alicia walked into the foyer.

"Thank you for speaking the truth," she said.

"There's more. That woman didn't write the letter. I did. That's just the way it works."

"Well, in the interests of full disclosure, I like a man with integrity, even if it takes him a while to show it."

I could move forward into this so easily. Her soft eyes just wanted a look from me, a word, to put it all into motion. But it was either too soon or too late.

"Can I drive you back to the office, or somewhere else?"

"Thanks, but I've got some writing to do. I'll just head to

a café for a while."

"More letters?"

"Yes."

"All right, but this offer doesn't come twice."

As I walked down the path and onto the sidewalk, my choice to leave Alicia made me feel nauseous. I walked to a café, and found a spot near the window. I had this idea about writing John Chande, to tell him how much his father loved him, to offer him some comfort in his grief. It would comfort me too, doing this. I did not want to hold on to Frank forever, just a while longer, just until it felt right to let him go.

The café door opened, letting in a rush of cold air that went up my pants. A young woman with a knapsack over one shoulder and skates over the other had come in. She stood at the entrance, waiting for her steamed-up glasses to defog so she could get her bearings. I felt the age-old pull, and forced myself to look away.

I worked on John's letter for a few hours. My fingers, so used to keyboarding, were out of practice with a pen, and I had to stop frequently to stretch out the cramps in my palm. More than that, I was so used to writing other people's words that I struggled to find my own. As the afternoon lengthened, words started to flow more easily, and I shifted my paper on the table to catch just the right amount of shadow and light.

MARK FOSS has worked for two foreign aid groups, and continues to write professionally about international development. His short fiction has appeared in *The New Quarterly*, *B&A New Fiction* and other Canadian literary journals since 1993. CBC broadcast his first radio drama in 2001.